ROUNDABOUTS

Also by Thelma Perkins

Wishing on a Wooden Spoon
In Search of Mr McKenzie: Two Sisters' Quest for an Unknown Father
(co-written with Isha McKenzie Mavinga)

Roundabouts

Thelma Perkins

MANGO PUBLISHING

2002

First published 2002

Published by Mango Publishing, London UK
P.O. Box 13378, London SE27 OZN
email: info@mangoprint.com
website: www.mangoprint.com

ISBN 1 902294 14 9

BLACK BRITISH SERIES

British Library Cataloguing in Publication Data
A CIP catalogue record for this book is available from the British Library

Printd in Great Britain by Creative Print and Design (Wales), Ebbw Vale

Cover design by Jacob Ross
Cover photograph by Teddy McKenzie and Pam Harris
Author portrait (back cover) by Natalie Perkins

Dedication

To those like my father who came before and to my parents who, although they didn't win, dared.

Thanks to Joan Anim-Addo for making this book possible and to my 'Sister' writers, members of the CWWA (Caribbean Women Writers' Alliance) support group, for their love, friendship, encouragement and curiosity.

1

'Hexscuse me, hexscuse me, Mistress.'

Doris looked around for the source of the voice. Surely that black man couldn't be calling to her. Looking straight ahead she quickened her pace, but he reached her side as she drew level with the zebra crossing. This time there was no mistaking that he was addressing her. Stepping back from the crossing, anxious that passing motorists shouldn't slow down for her, she faced him.

'Hexscuse me, Mistress.' His speech was quaint, formal. 'I'm trying to get to the Crystal Palace. They said to get on a P4 to Brixton and then a number 3 to the roundabout. Looks like I got off at the wrong roundabout. Can't see no Crystal Palace around here.'

Doris relaxed. The creases left her forehead, she lowered her shoulders that had been lifted defensively and loosened her clutch on the handles of her handbag. This old black man wearing gold rimmed glasses and a flat cap wasn't about to grab her bag and run. She half smiled to herself. If the truth were known she could probably run faster than him. For though he held himself erect, he carried a rubber-tipped walking stick.

'You got off the bus a little bit early, love.' The endearment slipped out unconsciously. Smiling, she turned and raised her free arm. Pointing upwards, she spoke again. 'Look, there's the transmitter, up the top of the hill. That's where the palace is. This roundabout is called Paxton Green.'

Side by side they stood looking around the green of the dog patch and over to the trees dominated by a stark steel structure.

'If you cross here with me, I'll show you where to catch the bus. 'Less you want to walk, that is?' Looking at his stick, Doris added, 'It's uphill all the way if you walk. Gypsy Hill's really steep and the other way is pleasant but just as hilly.'

'Hexercise is good for the body, so they say, but I would rather catch the bus and walk when I get there,' he replied. Seated on the wooden bench near the bus stop they sat apart viewing the red brick building of the health centre opposite. Doris broke silence.

'Where have you travelled from, then?'

Turning, Robert looked at her sitting at the other end of the bench. Her bag, held firmly by plump pink hands, rested lightly on her floral-covered knees. He smiled. On one finger of her right hand was a narrow gold band. She wore a navy hand-knitted cardigan that matched the pale blues and pinks of her cotton dress. Her hair was grey, short and wavy, nicely cut and smoothed back. Little curls clustered at the nape of her neck below which he could see the yellow clasp of her necklet. Clearing his throat he replied slowly,

'I live in Brockley, Mistress. I retired from the hospital after thirty years and I decided that I was going to see all the parks in London.'

His voice trailed off in case he had said too much. Then, almst apologetic, he added, 'Not a good start on me first day is it?' Before Doris could reply, the unmistakable roar of a London Routemaster was heard. They stood expectantly as it rounded the bend and she hastened towards the edge of the pavement, thrusting out her arm as she did so. 'It's this one, this one. Come on, get on.' Courteously he stood aside, then, without thinking, he followed her down the narrow aisle as the bus lurched up the hill and he sat down beside her. She half turned with a surprised look then smiled at him as she began to fumble in her bag murmuring, 'Bus pass, bus pass.' There they sat like any other couple taking a bus ride. Looking straight ahead, not speaking, not touching but very aware of each other. She pink and plump, a South Londoner born and bred. A pensioner, married, widowed, four children, four grandchildren. He mahogany skinned, arthritic hip, fingers gnarled from years of adjusting dusty boilers in basements. Jamaican born, veteran of the 'Empire Windrush' era. Father of four, a grandfather, he lived alone now with all the time in the world to fill. Time to visit London parks, a small consolation because he would never be able to afford to go back home, he thought.

He became aware of her perfume, a musty lavender, like the hedge in his little front garden. Where was she going?

'All change. Crystal Palace Park. Everybody off. All change, all change.'

The conductor's voice, insistent, gave no-one a chance to dream on, to ask questions, to dawdle even. They stood up as if pulled by strings and clutched the handrail of the seat in front of them. The bus stopped sharply throwing them together. He caught her arm and apologized immediately as he did so. She smiled back at him. His fingers felt soft and warm on the part of her arm where she habitually pushed up her sleeves. A fleeting touch of velvet. In that moment Doris changed her mind. Give Safeways a miss. How long was it since she had walked in a park?

He turned and held out a hand to help her from the bus and she accepted those fingers. This time she gripped them tightly, surprised at her boldness.

'This is the way to the park.'

Together they walked towards the roundabout with Doris now on the inside nearest to the peeling iron railings. The ground was strewn with litter: discarded tickets, travel passes, empty cigarette packs, burger boxes and drink cans. She looked at the overflowing litter bin and tutted. He empathized with her, 'If everyone took their rubbish home, no matter how small, this place wouldn't be like this. Everywhere you go it's the same and just look how many bins there are.'

They both paused to survey the pavement beside and before them. Around them people bustled. Everyone in their own world: rushing to catch a bus, to cross the road and catch another; to get to the newsagent in order to purchase a pass for a journey across London. Crystal Palace: a turning point, a meeting point. Four roads fanning out in different directions each to a different borough.

Connections to anywhere and everywhere. And the people hustling, bustling, unseeing, oblivious of the couple who had the whole day before them, a glorious sunny day on top of the world at Crystal Palace.

Robert needed his stick to keep up with Doris once she commenced the walk along the Parade. She pointed across the road to the shops: an assortment of old and refurbished cafes, a florist, a newsagent, a greengrocer and a hairdresser. 'That's where I get my hair done,' she said, lifting her arm and patting the back of her head. 'See those cafes? That's just the beginning. One day I walked round the whole Triangle. That's what we call this area. I counted all the places where you could get a meal. Over thirty of them there were. I ask you! But there are some shops in between. New ones too. A bit posh for me, though nice for those who can afford them. Look over there. This place needs new life. Not just cafes and pubs.' She stopped as they reached the top of the slight incline near a zebra crossing. Doris pointed again. 'Three pubs, one on each corner. Now you tell me, what do you want three pubs so close together for?' Turning left, she directed Robert towards the huge green and gold gates that led into the herb gardens. 'It's this way, love.'

The sun was warm. The gentle breeze ruffled her hair and dress. Robert and Doris sat on a slatted wooden bench slightly facing each other. The noise of the traffic and the occasional dog barking was interspersed with the shrieks of excited toddlers as they tried to escape the clutches of their minders.

'Would you like a mint?' He fumbled in the pocket of his cotton jacket to produce a packet of Polo mints. As she accepted one, Doris began to talk to him about what she knew of the park.

Walking along the terraces and down the wide, newly renovated steps, she guided him. Past the lakes and the concert bowl erected in readiness for summer evening concerts. The maze presented itself as a challenge, more for grandchildren than for an 'old man with a crook leg', she thought. Inquisitive squirrels watched as they journeyed along the asphalt paths bordered by rhododendrons and tall trees.

Nearing the end of an hour, they strolled down towards the tea house. Robert inclined his head while her soft voice told of the original glass palace, of the railway that brought people to the great exhibition, of the subway vault that could still be visited and the underground lines where rumour had it that a train full of dead people existed. They queued for a cup of tea, for sausage rolls and fruit tarts. Then they sat opposite each other beneath a striped parasol and quite formally introduced themselves. Like two Victorian statesmen they shook hands across the table.

'My name is Robert Williams. Pleased to meet you, Doris Thomas.'

The conversation flowed around themselves and their grandchildren. Doris saw hers often, Robert every weekend. Neither of them said much about their children. Then came the moment of realization. Here they sat, two pensioners, one white female, one black male, in a London park cementing a newly found friendship with the intimacies of family life. Doris leaned forward and placed her hand on the wooden tabletop. 'You know,' she said, 'I wasn't planning on spending a day in the park. I should have been going shopping.' Robert covered her hand with his.

'You changed your mind?' It was a question; not a statement.

'Why not?' she challenged. A pink spot appeared on each of her cheeks.

'I can go shopping any day but I might not meet a gentleman like you again.'

Now they were both laughing and for a brief moment their hands remained clasped, then Doris withdrew hers. Her forehead creased as she firmly folded her hands under the table. Robert's smile faded. He hadn't meant to cause offence. He cleared his throat and spoke in a gentle voice.

'Mistress Doris, I'm grateful that I got off the bus at the wrong stop. I was looking forward to walking in the park. Meeting you has made it even more pleasurable.'

Doris sniffed and sat upright. Her back seemed as stiff as it had been at the bus stop earlier.

Silence hung in the air between them. He didn't know what to do; how to continue. He waited. Surely touching her hand for the briefest of moments hadn't caused her that much offence? Doris lifted her cup and drained it. She placed it firmly on the saucer.

'I'm glad they use proper cups here. Can't bear those polywhatsit ones.' She picked up her handbag. 'Come on, it's a long way back to the gate and it's uphill all the way.'

Together they viewed the great stone dinosaurs while Doris, suddenly proud of her knowledge, spoke of what she knew. 'Did you know that once some people actually sat down inside one of them for a meal?' The names of the monsters were almost obliterated, making it virtually impossible to read what they were.

They entered the tiny zoo following groups of small children accompanied by adults. The main aim of the adults appeared to Doris to be that of keeping the children together, rather than allowing them to view the animals. The couple, silent now and wrapped in their own thoughts, gazed at the forlorn creatures in their cages and enclosures. Doris had been surprised by Robert taking her hand. She had felt a moment of confusion. Had she dealt with it appropriately, she wondered.

She could have snatched her hand away and spoken sharply. She could have even left him there at the table outside the cafeteria. A smile wreathed her face. Robert saw it. He said nothing. What, she wondered, was she doing walking around Crystal Palace park with a total stranger? Not only was he a black man, she was actually enjoying the walk. And she felt proud to be able to tell him something of the area. She thought suddenly that she would like to get to know him a little better.

Leaving the zoo they strolled beneath the trees towards the Sports Centre. Doris pushed to the back of her mind what her family's reaction would be if they knew that she fancied, just a tiny bit mind you, a black man.

'Robert.'

He stopped abruptly and leant on his stick, concern showing in his face. 'You all right, Mistress?'

'Oh yes, I'm all right, fine in fact. I was just thinking what a good idea this is of yours, to visit the parks, I mean. Would you like some company on your trips? Can I join you?'

Through June, July and August, Robert and Doris travelled London. In Kew Gardens Robert was able to point out the plants he remembered from his youth in Jamaica. They fed the squirrels in Greenwich Park, watched lovers dreaming in boats on the Serpentine, and picnicked on Hampstead Heath. They shared food carefully prepared by each other. Robert brought chicken, breadfruit salad and soft moist fried dumplings. Doris supplied salmon sandwiches, apple pies and great wedges of home-baked fruit cake. This prompted a discussion about the differences and similarities of food and fruit. Doris resolved to be more adventurous in her tastes. During the day in Hyde Park, they listened to a man extolling the virtues of the opposition party. They smiled at each other in embarrassment when one of the onlookers, using abusive language, began to harangue the orator. Together they sat and watched children being pushed back and forth on the swings in Victoria Park. And another day Doris brought bread for them to feed the ducks on the pond in Dulwich Park.

Eventually they found the tiny Postman's Park near London Wall where they read the tiles commemorating the brave deeds of postmen. And one afternoon they stood beneath Robert's huge striped umbrella in a grey drizzle more befitting November than July. It was in Battersea Park and they laughed then at the jugglers and mime artists.

Every Wednesday they journeyed backwards and forwards across London on the top of a swaying bus. When it rained they spent hours huddled in tea shops in the park before venturing homewards inside steamy vehicles crammed with tired commuters. One afternoon while attempting to cross a busy high street, Doris caught hold of Robert's hand as much for her own safety as his. Safe on the pavement, her hand remained in his. When he took her elbow to guide her onto a bus, Doris no longer felt a sense of outrage pass through her. She accepted his courtesy and returned it by putting her hand through his arm.

2

Robert's sons laughed when he told them he had a 'likkle' girlfriend.
Steven, the second eldest, assumed that he meant Priscilla, one of
the ladies who attended the local Church of God. A large,
formidable lady, Priscilla could pray with a voice that reached the
skies. She wore distinctive hats that always matched her outfits.
And the outfits she always designed and made herself. Ever since
Robert with his customary courtesy had rescued Priscilla from the
advances of a large dog outside the station, she had been pursuing
him not only for herself, but for God. She regularly invited him to
accompany her to prayer meetings. And when he declined, she
promised to pray for him. She made cakes for him. And on more
than one occasion, she had, using one pretext or another, managed
to get into his house to cook a meal.

'You finally given in to the church sister then, dad? What
was it, her cooking or the threat of eternal damnation?'

'Don't talk about the sister like dat, Steven. You know dat
she mean well. An no it not her.'

'Well who is it, then?' Aston asked. 'Someone from your club?'

On Tuesdays, Robert went to the local black pensioners club
where traditional Caribbean food was served. There he played
dominoes. Strictly men only. The women were excluded by design.
It was no accident that the men chose to sit in a window alcove
with their backs to the rest of the room. When Alice, the wife of
one of the men playing had, on several occasions, tried to join in,

they had called the game to a halt and made their excuses for leaving the table. Eventually, Alice gave up trying.

'No she not from the club and she not from the church.'

'Oh come on, daddy, stop teasing and tell us who she is.' Sharon, his youngest and only daughter sat down on the arm of his chair and put her arm around his neck.

'When you gonna get your hair cut, girl?'

Robert, proud of his daughter, could still not accept her growing her hair in dreadlocks. She had left school with enough examination passes to go to university. She was talented and attractive. It hardly seemed any time at all since he was chasing would-be boyfriends away from the door. Now in her late twenties she was a successful business woman, she drove a top of the range car had her own home, no partner and no babies. Robert made no attempt to hide his pride. He held her up as an example to his sons at each visit. He just wished that she hadn't got 'locks'.

'Never mind my hair, daddy. Tell us about this lady who you're bringing home tomorrow for dinner.'

Robert, who could not cut a long story short, began his explanation of where and how he had met Doris.

'What part of Jamaica she from, dad?' queried Aston.

'She not.'

'Well what island she from, then?' Steven, Aston and Sharon spoke in unison.

'She not.'

'Oh come on, now, dad. She not from back home? Oh, you wouldn't have an African girlfriend, would you?' Steven sounded irritated. 'And if she not from either, then she must be someone a lot younger than you because all the women your age wouldn't have been born here.'

'I never said she was African or from back home. I just said I had a likkle girlfriend an I wanted you to meet her. She live near Crystal Palace like I already told you.'

Robert hesitated in telling them that Doris was white. He didn't really know why. As a teenager, Steven had plenty of white girlfriends, some more serious than others. The group of friends he moved with always seemed to attract the girls as bees to nectar.

In the sixth form, Steven had discovered black consciousness and had become more interested in black history than in girls. Now his wife was a teacher. They had three children, all assertive and knowledgeable about their history. Aston, the quietest of his children, who had never shown any inclination towards black consciousness, still somehow gave the impression that he would disapprove of his father's relationship. Devon was in America. He didn't have to be told. And as for Sharon, well.

'Her name is Doris and she English, you know.'

'Dad does that mean she an old woman?' Steven demanded.

'What do you mean is she an ole woman?'

'Well there certainly aren't any young girls with a name like Doris.'

'What's your problem Steven, age or colour?' Robert sat upright in his chair. Sharon stood up and moved to sit opposite him.

'No problem, dad. I just can't see you with some little old white lady as a girlfriend.'

'Can you see me with a little old Jamaican woman, then? And besides, I said she was English. I didn't say anyting about she colour.'

'Dad.' Aston spoke now, 'We not looking an argument, you know. We just interested. You never mentioned anything about this woman before and now you telling us that she will be here for dinner tomorrow.'

'So make sure and come early for a change,' his father said.

Most Sundays Robert cooked for his family. He enjoyed being in the kitchen and it had become routine for his children and their families to arrive at some point during the afternoon ready for a traditional Caribbean Sunday lunch. If any of them were going elsewhere they would ring and let Robert know well before they knew he began the preparation. There was no set time to arrive or to eat.

'Food ready,' he would announce bringing in the first dish. The younger family members took that as a sign to lay the table and when everyone was seated, he asked who would 'grace' the table. Special occasions such as Christmas and birthdays, he went to one his children's homes.

'I didn't know I had to tell you what I did with me life.'

'You know you don't have to inform us, daddy,' said Sharon. 'I suppose it is because we never thought about you doing things without telling us and we never ever thought that you would have a girlfriend other than Sister Priscilla.'

'You never thought that I would have a white woman for a girlfriend either. White, black, ole, young, English, African, big or small island, church or not church is my business,' he answered.

'It's all right, dad.' Aston rose to leave. 'We aren't going to interfere in your life.'

'I hope she good to you, dad.' Steven winked at his father.

'You mind your business, man.' His father looked at him over the top of his glasses.

Later, as she was leaving, Sharon gave him a kiss and added her advice to that of her brothers.

'Mind she not after your money, daddy.' She smiled as she said it and left promising to be early the next day.

Robert went into the kitchen and began to cut up some chicken in readiness for the meal. 'Sister Priscilla me girlfriend indeed.' He enjoyed Doris's company. Now there was the difficulty of his children. He grew thoughtful as he worked and he wondered just how serious was their objection to the colour of his new friend.

3

Sunday dawned. A clear blue sky with a few puffs of white cloud drifting lazily towards the rising sun. More like spring than early autumn Robert reflected. He smiled to himself as he drew the curtains and looked out. He enjoyed working in the garden even if it did bother his hip a little, causing him to slow down or stop until the ache subsided. Both the apple tree and the pear tree were laden with fruit. Wallflowers and nicotiana stood upright opening up to the sun. Late roses peeped from among the different shades of green of the assorted shrubs dotted along the path.

Robert was sure that Doris would enjoy looking at his garden. Their conversation often stemmed from the gardens they looked at from the top deck of a bus. She confessed a love for roses though he understood that all flowers pleased her, especially scented ones. He spent the morning completing the preparations begun the previous evening. Only then did he go into his garden to select and pick a bunch of roses to complement the carefully laid table. He was taking no chances on the grandchildren laying the table incorrectly today.

Standing back he surveyed his handiwork. The cloth was snowy white set with the cork table mats and gleaming cutlery, his best set, only brought out at Christmas. Beside every place mat lay a linen napkin. Usually the family made do with paper ones. The roses sat pride of place in the centre, their sweet musky scent filling the room. Surrounding the vase were empty mats awaiting the dishes which Robert had spent the morning cooking. Only the salad to prepare now, then he would take a quick shower, dress and go to the bus stop where he had arranged to meet Doris.

Robert's heart beat a little faster than usual. He felt a sudden anxiety about bringing her to his home. After the children left the night before, he had brought out the vacuum cleaner and done the carpets again. The already polished furniture was dusted, too, and the hand towel in the small downstairs toilet checked. He tried to tell himself that bringing Doris to his home presented no problems. His apprehension lay in her meeting his family. Yet all the while he argued that surely his children would be happy for him that he had a found a woman friend after the years spent bringing them up alone.

How would they treat her and what would she think of his family? Standing at the bus stop waiting, he fidgeted first with his tie, then with the zipper on his jacket. His hands moved from tie to zipper to pockets in an effort to still them. He was sure the gas was turned off beneath the rice. Suppose there was too much pepper in the gravy that was to accompany the fried chicken. Did she say she liked sweet peppers or not? He hoped the potatoes left roasting in the oven would be okay.

The plan was that he would meet Doris and take her home to get her settled and comfortable before the family arrived. A bus came and went straight past without slowing down. His eyes strained to see if she was standing on it. The bus stop was a request. Perhaps she hadn't stood up in time or rung the bell early enough. Half an hour passed. Robert looked at his watch again. The children were to be at the house in less than twenty minutes.

He began to pace up and down. Because the stop was just around the corner from his house he had come out leaving his stick at home. Now the walking, coupled with the feeling of misapprehension, was making his leg ache. Leaning against a wall several yards from the bus stop, he looked again at his watch. He began making excuses to himself for her nonappearance. Ten minutes more then he would have to return home.

If she did not come, argued Robert, that could signal the end of the weekly outings because he did not know where to contact her. He did not have her address or her telephone number. Hearing the sound of another bus, Robert limped towards the stop. He peered with some trepidation towards the exit doors. Was she there? His heart leapt when her face appeared and he moved forward to offer his hand as she stepped down. But his smile soon faded when, after greeting him, she explained the reason for her being late.

Her daughter had telephoned just as she was leaving the house. Her grandson, Billy, the eldest one, had been taken to hospital with appendicitis.

'They want me to look after his sister until they return from the hospital. I'm so sorry, Robert. I really am.'

There was nothing she could do. She didn't have his telephone number so she couldn't call. She knew he would be waiting and that's why, after having agreed, she had told them that she would make her own way to the hospital to collect the little one.

'I just didn't want to leave you in the lurch.'

Robert did not know what to say. There was nothing he could say and Doris saw the disappointment in his face. She felt mortified.

'There will be a next time, dear.' She caught his hand and looked directly into his eyes. 'Now, I remember you telling me about a cab office near here.'

Robert nodded miserably trying to find his voice. Clearing his throat he managed to offer to walk with her to the mini-cab office where, before he saw her into the waiting car, they planned when and where their next meeting was to be. He fumbled about in his jacket pocket for a piece of paper on which to write his telephone number. All he could find was a crumpled wrapper from a packet of mints. Smoothing it out he used the proffered pencil that Doris produced from her bag and wrote down his number. The car sped away.

He began to walk homeward. He walked slowly, stopping every few yards to lean against a wall. 'Fool ting yu done dere Robert, yu neva aks for her telephone number even though she got yours.'

4

They sat together watching a mother duck followed by her half grown ducklings into the still waters of the pond. Neither of them spoke as first the mother then the eight brown and white youngsters took to the water, their webbed feet scarcely causing a ripple. As they neared the centre of the pond, Robert broke the silence.

'Strange how ducks can walk an swim an dey dont have no lessons at all.' He half turned to Doris, 'We take time to begin to walk an dose who can swim all have to have lessons first off.' Doris nodded in agreement, remembering the Saturday mornings spent at the swimming baths watching her children being guided through the arm and leg movements, the correct way to breathe and hold their heads. Then, once they could swim, she used to take them to the baths at Dulwich on Sunday mornings only too pleased to spend an hour in the water with them. As the children grew more independent and began to go out with their own friends, her visits to the baths ceased. She could not think how long it had been since she had swum a length. Her costume must be full of moth holes.

'Robert,' she took his hand as she so often did nowadays when she began to talk with him. It was a totally unselfconscious action that developed as they rode on buses discussing the sights as they travelled around London. She would take his hand and hold it clasped between both of hers and there they rested on either her knee or his. Sometimes her hand gently stroked the back of his, her warm, soft, fingertips tracing the work-hardened brown whorls of the joints before travelling towards his straight cut nails and stubby fingertips.

Considering her reaction that first time he held her hand, it had taken Robert a little while to become accustomed to the idea that she now appeared so comfortable with him that she usually made the first move. Whenever he reached for her hand, he always glanced at her face to check for a reaction.

'How about us going swimming one day?'

'I haven't been swimmin since me was a likkle, likkle boy. An den it was always in de river.'

'What about when your children were small, didn't you ever take them?'

He recalled his children asking for money at weekends and occasionally during the summer holidays in order to accompany their friends to the local pool. He'd never taken them, neither was he aware of them having had lessons other than the routine ones during school time. Occasionally certificates were flashed at him and then stuck on the fridge door only to disappear, never to be seen again as far as he knew.

'Would do your hip the world of good, you know.'

Doris noticed that some days Robert would lean more heavily on his stick while denying that he was in any pain as he struggled to climb a hill or mount the step of a bus. He told her that it was arthritis and that he was 'on the list' for an operation but didn't know how long it would be.

Robert grunted, unconvinced. 'I hear dat de water in dem pools is cold an me certainly not going swimmin in cold water.'

'Oh no it isn't,' exclaimed Doris. 'Well it never used to be. I'll tell you what, next time we plan to go out and it's raining, let's go for a swim instead. I'll check out the pools and find out where the water is kept at a reasonable temperature. What do you think?'

Robert was noncommittal.

Standing in front of her wardrobe mirror wearing her old swimsuit, Doris surveyed her body. She turned left, then right, then executed a full circle. Finally, she stood very still to review her full frontal reflection. 'Mmm, I have certainly put on some weight since

I last wore this,' she mused. Running her hands down over her stomach, she drew in her breath trying to reduce the slight but obvious protuberance pushing against the navy and white spotted fabric that was worn thin and in danger of breaking into holes.

It must have been about two or three years before Frank died when she'd last worn the costume. They'd gone to Cornwall in late June. The preceding spring had been unusually warm and if her memory served her right, even the sea had been welcoming. After swimming idly in the water, they had each lain on the beach immersed in a book of their own. The costume was about six years old, then. No wonder it had disintegrated, hanging in the wardrobe all this time.

When she went on holiday with the family she never swam. The assumption was that she was responsible for keeping an eye on the children. Her place was beneath the huge umbrella on the beach dispensing cold drinks, rubbing on sun lotion, supervising excavations and settling arguments over spades, buckets, empty cartons, sticks or shells.

Sitting down on the bed, Doris looked at her white thighs, mottled with blue veins that spread and joined together resembling streams and rivers on an ordnance survey map. She was still facing her reflection. Lifting her head, she reviewed her neck. Her eyes travelled along with her hands over her breasts. Still firm, they felt and looked good enclosed in the uplift of her swimsuit. She rested her hands lightly on her stomach and wondered what Robert would think when he saw her for the first time in a state of undress. He was such a gentleman, so polite and courteous. Gentle really was the right word for him.

Never could she have imagined a black man being so softly spoken or as caring as Robert appeared to be. All the images she had held in her head were those presented by the media. Or, they were based on how she saw young people acting on public transport and on the street. Whenever her grandson and his friend visited they always spoke loudly. Their movements were exaggerated, fast; they were never still for a moment except when involved with a computer game. Then, their eyes and hands were the only parts of them involved. And even then speed was essential. Perhaps it was only the young who were loud and yes, to some extent, rude. Her own children were always in a hurry these days to do things, go places, acquire objects. They were not always gentle either. They often demonstrated impatience with her and their own children. Was it only as one grew old that those qualities developed? Come to think of it, until now there had been very few elderly black people on the streets as far as she could recall. Now, like Robert, they were retiring after years of working, trying to catch that elusive star. Now they had time to walk, talk, join clubs and socialize without having to watch the clock.

Her thoughts turned to her own husband and whether he had been a gentle man. He had not always been patient. At times he had treated her as if she was simply not as intelligent as he. Her place was at home with the children. He never credited her with being able to understand politics. For example, he had always told her who she should vote for, but not why. True, he took care of all the bills and when he died after a sudden massive stroke, she hadn't even known about insurance policies, bank accounts or how to write a cheque. She learnt then very quickly to manage financial matters for herself. Sitting on her bed reflecting on her past, she realized how few mistakes she had made. 'I would have been all right with a little job,' she thought. Now it was too late for work, but it wasn't too late for some pleasure with a companion who treated her as an equal. That was it. Frank had never treated her as an equal. His wife. The mother of his children. Only a housewife, never a woman. Robert treated her as a woman.

How would he react when he saw her looking like this in a swimming costume? Doris stood up, raised her arms and reached to lower her straps. She pulled down the worn fabric and slowly uncovered her breasts and then her stomach. She stepped out of the suit and stood perfectly still.

'Why do you want some swim shorts, daddy?' Sharon stood, hands in pockets, smiling down at him as he counted some notes out of his wallet.

'Is none o yu business, but if yu mus know me goin start to go swimmin wid me friend.'

'What friend, daddy? I thought that your friends only liked to play cards and dominoes.'

'Well yu thought wrong, den, didnt yu? Mi did tell yu bout her awready. Yu know dat we go together to different places. Well, she suggest dat swimmin is good fi mi bad leg.'

Robert's chin jutted out defiantly. Since the Sunday when Doris's place at the dining table remained empty, his children had carefully avoided the subject of female friends. They assumed that his weekly outings were solitary. Suddenly as she realized what he had said Sharon sat down.

'Who you said you going swimming with, daddy?' She leaned forward on the edge of her seat.

'Yu gonna get me some swim shorts or will I have to aks de boys dem?'

Okay, daddy. But I can't do it before Saturday. And you can come with me and choose them yourself. But you said *she*.'

Her father smiled at her and then as if he didn't want the furniture to hear, because there was no-one else in the house, he lowered his voice.

'Yu remember de lady I tole yu bout long time back. The one who should a come to dinner dat Sunday an didnt mek it? We been goin on a bus ride every week. She tink swimmin would do me bad leg good. So me gonna try it. Dat's all.'

Sharon knew from experience that by the way in which he concluded the sentence, she was not to ask any more questions. She persisted.

'You never told us that you had been able to contact her again, daddy. You really are a crafty old horse managing to keep her to yourself. How long has this been going on?'

'Never yu mind,' he said, turning from her and pressing his lips together in a firm straight line. He had never confided his business to his children and he wasn't about to start now.

Robert had given the idea of going swimming a great deal of thought. As a boy growing up in Jamaica, he had learned to swim in the river not far from his home. Along with other local boys, he'd leapt and bounded from rock to rock finally leaping into the warm flowing water and floundering about until somehow he had begun to swim. Just like the older boys among the group, he was suddenly able to propel himself along, without his feet touching the bottom and without struggling to keep his mouth, nose and eyes free from water. He remembered how most of them swam, a strong sideways crawl, one eye always on the lookout for an adult coming to bawl them out of the water.

Time at the river was a pleasure that you earned. Chores had to be done first. Errands had to be run after school was over. Then shouting, leaping, pushing, they would go barefoot in old shorts naked from the waist up towards the river. Only boys; never the girls. And until now he had never questioned why never the girls.

As a teenager he'd been quite a strong swimmer but since his arrival in England he'd never swum. Sharon, who often arrived with items of clothing for him, bought because she either thought he needed them or they would suit him, was surely the best person to help him with his purchase of swimming shorts. Only now he was beginning to notice the long absence of a woman in his life.

There hadn't been many girlfriends either, before the mother of his children. And after she left, he steered clear of them. But he had always treated her like a queen. Because that was what he had considered her to be. He married her when he could have lived with her. He struggled to buy her whatever she wanted. He let her continue to work after the children arrived. It was he who had taken the children to the minder. He had run from work to home to check that they had been collected; run from home to the minder apologizing for being late again because he thought that their mother had collected them that fateful day. He had never raised his hand to her, never shouted at her, never even looked at other women after he met her. And just like that she had left him.

Just didn't come home one day after work. Telephoned a week later after he had searched the hospital, police station, you name it. Said she wasn't coming back. Didn't love him, didn't want the children, the house, anything. He could have it all.

And now there was Doris; after all this time, a woman in his life. He recalled the day he told his sons. They had treated it as a joke. Sharon didn't seem to mind. He pondered on what Doris's thoughts might be when she saw him undressed; saw his slightly stooped shoulders, the white hairs on his chest, the belly that just wouldn't keep the elastic of the swim shorts up on top. There were the knees scarred from boyhood accidents, the bowed leg that had developed because of his hip trouble. Most of all, what would she think of his blackness? She never mentioned his colour when they were out together but she always held his hand now.

Robert took a quick shower and left the changing room to walk out to the poolside where Doris was already waiting for him in her new costume. She smiled encouragingly watching him walk gingerly towards her. She feared that he might slip on the shining wet surface as he no longer had his stick as a support.

'Come,' she said, guiding him towards the steps. 'This is the shallow end and the water is lovely.'

Slowly he lowered himself into the clear blue water and let go of the handrail. Doris was already swimming up the length of the pool. He struck out after her, swimming the way he had done all those years ago in the river, a sideways crawl that took him effortlessly along. And there was no pain.

Afterwards, they sat at a red formica-topped table drinking tea, both with hair still damp and eyes tingling from the effects of the chemicals. Robert told her shyly that he admired the way she looked in her swimsuit and how well she swam. She reciprocated with compliments about his style of swimming and his attractive swimming trunks.

The air was charged with their unspoken thoughts. Deep down inside her, Doris felt something stir. Something akin to that first flutter of life, the first movement of a growing baby's first kick. Alike, she thought, but not the same. The sensation sent, not a feeling of awe and wonder to her brain, but a thrill of excitement straight to her heart. For one brief moment she thought she might be having a heart attack. This must be what it feels like, she thought. Except I don't want to die just yet, please God. Not now.

5

As the late summer drew to a close, both Robert and Doris recognised that the weekly visits to outdoor venues would end. The evenings were drawing in and it was usually dark before either of them reached home. Each week as they sat in a cafe, or picnicked beneath a tree they studied the brochure giving details of the parks and open spaces in and around London. The leaflet was well worn, creased and crumpled despite being carefully folded back into a plastic wallet after use.

Robert had found it in his local library one afternoon when he had gone to renew his books. That was another good thing about retirement, he remembered thinking. Now he had all the time in the world to read. There was a time when the children were younger, when, even paperback books had been beyond his pocket. Instead he used the local library and encouraged the children to do the same. 'If you read, you get the knowledge,' he would say. 'An if you want to find out about something an nobody can tell you what it is you want to know, look in de books dem an you will surely find it.' His daughter had taken her cue from him and was always reading. Books everywhere. All the time. Somehow she was able to read several books simultaneously. There was one beside her bed. One she carried around with her to read on trains and buses. That was before she drove. And if it were possible to drive and read she would be doing it. There was often a book in the toilet. Though when all the children still lived at home, no-one stood a chance of staying in there long enough to read more than a couple of pages. And many times Robert retrieved from the floor in the bathroom a paperback, its cover limp, its corners curling with damp. He quarreled with her then about not looking after the books, particularly if they were not hers.

Of his sons, only Steven had continued to read after leaving the junior school. One evening soon after his thirteenth birthday, when another open evening at school had ended with Robert informing the teacher that his own expectations for his children were obviously higher than those of the school, Steven told him how he missed the teachers sharing books and stories with them as they had done in the junior school. Out of that conversation had grown the habit of passing books between himself and his son.

Aston had begun to read for pleasure when he was fifteen. Much to his father's surprise. After a severe bout of flu which confined him to the house, he began to browse through one of Steven's books. Very quickly he discovered black authors and from then on, there was no stopping him. Sometimes Sunday dinner would turn into an earnest literary discussion where Robert occasionally felt out of his depths. Still, the seeds were sown with good results. He only wished he could afford to buy books. He would have dearly loved to leave a library to his grandchildren.

The parks' leaflet was the turning point out of a gradual depression that had begun to descend on him as the date for his retirement drew near. Going to the club could help to fill the void left, following a lifetime of days working from eight to six, five days a week. But he really didn't want to spend every day playing dominoes and discussing cricket scores with old men! The church ladies would have also found ways to use up his empty hours, doing good deeds and repairing the building. So after gathering up all the free brochures on the information table and carrying them home in the plastic carrier bag along with the books, he had been pleasantly surprised as he read and the idea of visiting the parks began to grow. During the evening he had returned to the booklet and begun to plan his summer.

Now here he was sitting with Doris in Richmond Park finishing off the remains of their lunch and thinking about the coming winter. Everywhere were signs of autumn. The ground was covered with yellow and orange leaves that sighed and shifted as a skittish little breeze blew through the almost bare branches of the trees. The patches of fern were turning to a russet brown and squirrels darted about selecting acorns and beechnuts for their winter store. There was a damp smell in the air mingled with wood smoke. Both Robert and Doris wore jackets.

With a sigh, he turned to her and said, 'I can't see us doin much more of this, can you?'

Doris shook her head. She carefully wiped her mouth with a tissue to remove any cake crumbs from the corners.

'I am really going to miss the outings, you know. I thought about the museums and places like that but we might have to pay to get in.'

Robert was silent for a moment. He folded his own napkin and replaced it inside the lunchbox. Taking a sip of lukewarm coffee, he shifted his position to ease the dull ache in his hip.

'What you tink about goin swimmin each week?'

Doris looked at him in surprise. He hadn't mentioned going since that first time. She had thought that perhaps he hadn't enjoyed it as much as he said.

'I like meetin with you every week. Besides, it might help to make the winter go faster.'

'Oh Robert.' Her voice was tremulous. 'I was wondering what to do once it got too cold for our outings. And I have so looked forward to these days.' She was amazed at herself. Was it really her voice sounding like one of those silly starlets in an old film? She couldn't ever remember her voice being affected this way before. She cleared her throat in an effort to get rid of the tremor. When she continued, she imagined she sounded a little better.

'How about trying different swimming baths until we find one we really like? A bit like us going to different parks each week. Most of the boroughs operate a free scheme for pensioners which means that we could continue the journeys using our passes.'

Robert was silent. His hip had been very painful of late. He knew that the swimming was good therapy. The problem was walking and getting on and off buses. Once or twice during the last few weeks Doris had reached out and steadied him as he struggled to negotiate a way off the bus. He was embarrassed, and always apologised for some minutes afterwards. His doctor was supposed to be contacting the hospital consultant to find out how much longer he would have to wait before being given a new hip.

'In the meantime'. The doctor looked at him over the rim of her glasses in an old fashioned sort of way. 'Keep as mobile as you can. Gentle exercise every day, walking, swimming things like that.'

He nodded, wondering where a young thing like her had acquired such an old fashioned habit. Mind you, he thought sometime later, she couldn't be that young, not to be a doctor. She had a family, too. There was a photograph of them on her desk.

'Robert.' Doris brought him back to the park. 'If that's what you want to do, let's give it a try. Sounds like a good alternative to parks in the winter, anyway.'

Neither of them spoke for a while, each deep in thought, watching the leaves scurrying across the grass. Content with each other's company, there was no need for words. Doris was reminded of a poem she had heard once, she couldn't remember where she had learnt it or who it was by. Something about leaves.

'Leaves fall, unheard, though seen.'

Then there was a bit about colours and growing old and changes. She cast about in her mind for the next lines. If she could remember them she knew the whole poem would come to her. There were some lines about shuffling and rustling which made her think of Robert sitting beside her on the small rug. On the days when his leg was particularly painful he shuffled a bit and right now he was rustling about in the lunch box, though not tidying up and putting everything back in its place as she tended to do. 'Shuffled by feet.' Rustling feet or creaking feet? she puzzled.

'What are you looking for?'

The poem was temporarily pushed aside.

'Where's me little knife? I got somting for you, if it not squashed in de bottom of de bag.'

Doris lifted the corner of a paper napkin and produced the penknife that he had used earlier. He took a mango from the front pocket of his backpack and held it in the palm of his hand. Turning to her he offered it. She was aware of the slight movement of the dark fingers that lay outstretched. A perfect match for the orange and yellow-hued fruit. The suspended poem came to her and she held it there on her tongue, in her head as the sweet perfume of the golden orange fruit assailed her.

'Leaves fall, unheard, though seen,
Shades of red, orange, yellow,
Once were green.'

She knew what the fruit was having seen them when she shopped in Brixton market, the nearest shopping centre to her home. But she had never eaten one and didn't quite know what to do when she took it from him. Raising it, she sniffed the smooth skin. Did she know Robert well enough to ask him how it should be eaten?

'You ever had one?'

She shook her head.

'Come'.

As Doris watched, she recalled the poem:

'Sere, brittle, rustling in the wind.
Shuffled by feet,
Rustling,

Shuffling feet,
Creaking bones.
Autumn comes quietly,
Silently, felt, seen,
Companioned with memories,
Once were green.'

He took the mango from her and deftly sliced off one side. Carefully laying down the remaining fruit, he proceeded to take the knife back and forth across the tear shaped, peach coloured slice that nestled in the palm of his hand. Not quite through to the skin but close enough so that when he carefully pulled the skin back, the cubes of fruit stood out glistening as the juice emerged between the carved lines.

'Borne in the wind,
On the breath of sighs.
Seasonal, cyclical, passage of time.'

Her eyes were drawn to his fingers as they carved the succulent flesh.

'Black, yellow, burnished, bronze,
Fading grey to white.
Dry, brittle bones
Stir slow towards night.'

He proffered the mango, and Doris again caught the rich scent that she couldn't quite name.

'Eat it like this,' he said, lifting it to her mouth. 'Jus bite de cubes off wid your teeth. Go on.'

Doris sank her teeth into the moist flesh. No crunch or crackle, her teeth slid across the skin. The flesh left its anchor. Her whole face received the scent as the cubes melted on her tongue and juice trickled down her chin. She bit again and again until the skin was bare and only then was she aware of the juice on her face and down her neck.

'Here.'

Robert was offering the other side to her. There was no prompting from him this time. Trying to find words to describe the feeling inside her as her taste buds awoke, she ate. And after, Robert gently took a tissue and began to wipe her mouth and chin as delicately as he would a baby's. Once again that same stirring moved deep inside her like a long lost memory.

'Rustling leaves, shuffling feet.'

She could hear them.

'After autumn, winter sleep.'

From a long way off she heard someone sigh and with the sigh she felt her body release, relax. She lifted her hands to his face and gently, gently drew it towards her own. Mango kisses, kisses the scent and the flavour of tropical fruit. His lips were as soft as the sigh that had left her breathless and in that instant Doris died and breathed anew again bathed in juices of the Caribbean. Slowly, slowly they parted and almost embarrassed, without looking at each other, they began to tidy away the remnants of the picnic.

From her bag Doris took a 'Wet Wipe' to remove the last sticky remnant. She offered one to Robert.

Standing, she straightened her skirt and reached out her hand to help Robert up. As he came level with her, they shyly kissed again. And after the kiss, they stood momentarily chest to chest feeling each other's heart beat and their breathing as one.

Robert and Doris walked hand in hand towards the gates of the park. The wind strengthened. Leaves scurried. Wood-scented smoke drifted across the browning bracken. Doris sniffed. 'There must still be some juice on my clothes', she thought as her feet rustled the mango coloured leaves.

6

Throughout the months that followed, Doris lived from one Wednesday with Robert to another. The days in between were filled with anticipation. She marvelled at her ability to keep her weekly outings a secret from her family and also from her friends at the club. Keeping that secret was both painful and pleasurable. Painful because there were times when she wanted to share her experiences and discuss her feelings with another woman. At night she lay awake asking herself questions, unable to find solutions. The feeling that arose when she and Robert touched. That kiss in the park. The sadness she experienced when they said goodbye and the overwhelming joy that flooded her whole being each time she saw him approaching.

She was always early, always first, sitting in the corner close to the steamy glass, watching, waiting. Anyone watching them saw a mixed race couple, elderly, not old. And they liked each other, liked each other's company, liked being together. That was all there was to it, she argued.

Having a secret felt childish. Yet Doris enjoyed her secret. She derived a simple pleasure in keeping her secret from her friend Amy and, she had to admit, from her own family. Amy was curious about why Doris now only attended the lunch club one day a week. Doris hugged herself when she recalled Amy's questions and how she managed to evade them. Her evasiveness, she knew, irritated Amy who came a close second to Joan, her eldest daughter, in the busybody stakes. If Amy was different, she might have talked with her about her emotions. If her daughter was different she might have talked with her about Robert. If Robert was white; if he was not black.

Robert, too, also looked forward to Wednesdays even though there were days when his hip caused him to grumble and mutter out aloud, glad that he was alone in the house and that no-one could hear him cursing the pain as he rubbed in liniment, swallowed painkillers, struggled into his trousers and bent painfully to fasten his shoes, polished to a shine that reflected his grimaces of the previous evening.

Travelling to the Palace - Crystal Palace - his backpack balanced on his knees, he anticipated her smile, saw the excited wave, heard the impatient rap on the glass if he didn't respond immediately to her greeting. Unlike Doris, his mind was not crowded with questions. His children no longer asked him or teased him with queries about his girlfriend. Sharon occasionally asked him if the swimming was doing any good and the boys mentioned Sister Priscilla from time to time. Sister Priscilla herself continued to waylay him at the club or outside the church when he passed just as she was entering or leaving. She was comforted by the fact that 'One day brudder Robert, de lawd gwan answer me prayers.'

Being with Doris brought a light into his life in a way that Sister Priscilla described living with her Jesus. It didn't cross his mind that what he felt for Doris was love. He had pushed love into a corner many years ago, determined not to be hurt again. Instead he had concentrated on raising his family. And his demonstrations of affection were restrained except with his grandchildren whose exuberance was difficult to resist.

The waiters, Michel, Francois and Anne-Marie often speculated between themselves about the pair of pensioners who met on Wednesday mornings in their cafe. Obviously they were not married, because they never arrived together, declared Michel. Francois was sure that they were married (but not to each other), and were having an affair. Anne-Marie thought that they were old friends who had met again after many years but could not be seen in their own locality because of the scandal. 'What scandal?' asked Michel. 'Isn't it obvious?' Anne-Marie responded. 'He is a black man and she is not black.' 'Non, non it is because they are old people,' said Michel. 'But old people do not have to hide from their acquaintances', interjected Anne-Marie nudging Francois in his ribs with her elbow as Robert pushed his way through the door and made his way to the corner table. Doris, her face alight with pleasure, greeted him.

Francois tucked his red and white teatowel into the back of his apron before walking across to them. Bending towards Doris he caught the smell of lavender.

'Two teas, madame?'

They both nodded.

'And your usual pastries?'

Robert and Doris nodded again. Francois noted that they both had bags with them.

'Perhaps they contained toiletries and nightclothes,' he reported back to his colleagues. He added, 'maybe they go off and spend a day in a hotel.'

'Do you think they would come here first if they were going to spend a day in a hotel bedroom?' whispered Michel.

Doris and Robert were going swimming at the leisure centre in South Norwood. Winter was fast approaching bringing cold grey days and freezing nights that dawned with clear blue skies, icy winds and treacherous frosts. Twice already Robert had been forced to abandon local shopping trips, fearful that he would slip on the frost-covered pavements. There was one late November morning when Doris had waited in vain for a number three bus to take her to Herne Hill to the lunch club. She had huddled into a corner of the bus shelter as the wind buffeted the sides until she thought it would be lifted from its foundations.

All night long the wind blew, reminding her of childhood stories where it first moaned, then howled, trying to enter every crevice of the woodland cottage where the heroine lived. She'd pulled her quilt over her head, trying to blot out the whistling, the thudding and the sounds of objects being hurled in fury up and down the road. Eventually a passing neighbour informed her that a tree was lying across the South Croxted Road and no buses could get through. Doris made her way home relieved that it wasn't a Wednesday. Now two weeks before Christmas they were off on the last outing of the year having agreed to meet again at the Cafe on the third Wednesday in January, weather permitting.

'I know it is difficult for you when it is frosty.' Doris patted his hand, sealing their agreement before they both stood in readiness to leave the cafe.

The previous week they journeyed by bus to the South Bank where free lunchtime concerts were held regularly. They were fortunate enough to arrive early and secure seats. A visiting steelband performed a medley of familiar television theme tunes mixed with calypsos and favourite love songs. Robert tapped his foot in time to the rhythm and Doris hummed along contentedly, her hand clasped in his. Following the concert they treated themselves to scones and hot chocolate before catching a bus back to Crystal Palace.

Robert, although irritated by his lack of mobility was soon immersed in his usual preparations for a family Christmas. He discussed each grandchild's present with Sharon. 'I cant walk all around dem shops, girl, wid dis leg de way it is. So, yu get de tings for me, an find out what mi should get your brudders dem.'

'Okay, daddy, but I hope that by this time next year you will have that leg sorted out and be able to get about more easily.'

'I jus want to be free of de dyamm ache all o de time.'

As for Doris, her eldest daughter took over her life as usual, checking that she had made the Christmas puddings, was available for child minding when necessary and knew the routine for Christmas family visits. She also provided Doris with a list of suitable presents and clear instructions not to spend too much money, 'because the children have enough as it is.'

The weather prevented Robert and Doris from meeting until mid-February. A heavy snowfall during the second week of January left most of the south east covered in a thick blanket of snow that froze solid, causing traffic delays, accidents and shutdowns. Neither Robert nor Doris ventured out, both being fortunate enough to have a family to shop and run errands for them. Robert tolerated his, while Doris railed against being told what she could and couldn't do. She longed for a break in the arctic conditions. Not only to release her from her tyrannical daughter, but also so that she could once again have her outings with Robert.

Although it was still very cold, a watery sun had succeeded in melting the overnight frost. Drops of melting ice pooled on grey paving slabs as Robert leaning on his stick, walked gingerly from the bus stop towards the cafe. Anne-Marie, Michel and Francois gave each other the thumbs up sign when he entered. They had been anxiously watching the door for the past fifteen minutes, ever since Doris had seated herself in her regular corner. All three had missed the couple and agreed that the weather must have affected their assignations. The stories they wove around Robert and Doris coloured the long hours spent in the little cafe serving French snacks, coffee and milk shakes. Now with winter over, they heaved an almost audible sigh of relief with Robert's appearance. She had not been abandoned by him!

They stayed in the cafe that first morning, making two cups of tea each last two hours. Holding hands across the table, each told the other tales of the previous weeks. The cafe staff watched. They smiled and whispered to each other, unperturbed by the lack of orders. Each was busy with their own version of a love story they would tell later that day. Meanwhile Robert and Doris planned a visit to the cinema, another outing to the South Bank, a swim and as soon as possible a first visit to a park.

7

Doris was trying to remember when she last felt so happy and contented as she did right now, sitting on a bench beside Robert in the sunken rose garden, part of the Horniman Museum complex. There may have been times before she met Robert, she thought, but they were in the far distant past. Almost in another life. Yes that was it. This is a new life, apart and different from anything I have known before, she told herself. What an ordinary life I have led. There must be millions of women in this country whose existence is exactly the same as mine used to be. Married in the late fifties to an ex-soldier who left the army and worked in the same job for forty years. Buying a little house, having three or four children, staying at home, being a housewife. That's a strange word too. When I look back I suppose I was married to my house. He went to work while I cared for our children and the house. Everything was so routine. Monday to Friday, school, shopping, cleaning, shopping, cleaning, school. Saturday and Sunday, cleaning the car, going for a drive with the children forever arguing in the back. Breakfast, dinner, tea, bed, breakfast, dinner, tea, bed. Round and round and round. Bed.

Flat on my back looking at the ceiling while Frank grunted, panted and groaned, squeezed my breasts, choked me with his tongue, grunted, panted and groaned some more, turned over and went to sleep. Did he ever tell me he loved me? I suppose he must have done. But I can't remember.

Like most of her school friends, Doris had known Frank all her life. Infant school, junior school, seeing him from a distance lounging as a young teddy boy in a gang on the corner when she passed with her friends on the way home from secondary school. Working in the office of Morley's department store when she left school at fifteen. Meeting Frank again at the youth club. Nights slapping his hands away when they kissed in the back row of the picture house. Writing faithfully once a week when he was called up to do his national service. Getting engaged one weekend while he was on leave when she was just eighteen and marrying him soon after he was demobilised. And that was it. My life. Nothing to talk about, nothing to write about. I wonder if I was happy. I suppose I was, then, because that was the way life was. No adventure, no expectations, no romance.

Ah, that's what I have now. Romance and adventure and happiness. Does Robert love me? Do I love Robert? He hasn't told me that he loves me. Nevertheless I like him very, very much. I could tell him. But.

'What yu tinking about, Doris?'

'What? Pardon? Sorry. I was miles away.'

'Me was wonderin what yu was tinkin about. Sitting dere wid dat far away look in your eyes.'

She wondered if she should tell him. If telling him would spoil what they had.

'It is just heavenly sitting here like this, in this beautiful garden, being here with you.'

'An de weatherman been kind to us again, eh?'

That was true. Since April they had been lucky so far. Only once had it rained on a Wednesday. Even if rain fell Monday or Tuesday, Wednesday would dawn bright and clear.

'Someone is watching over us,' thought Doris.

She wasn't a religious person. A Christian, yes, but not religious.

Her white wedding, held in St Stephen's church, the christenings of her children in the same church by the same vicar who had married them. They were religious occasions, with hymns, favourites learned in primary school, and prayers including 'The

Lord's Prayer'. Christian ceremonies. Traditional, expected. Even Frank's funeral service was a religious affair conducted by a vicar who looked barely old enough to have left school. Perhaps in her old age somebody somewhere was looking kindly on her and had decided that in the afternoon of her life she should know happiness and maybe even real love.

The park was equidistant from both of their homes so instead of meeting at the French cafe on the parade, where the staff now regarded them as regulars, though quaint ones, they met outside the park gates and began a slow journey around. Wherever they went and whatever park they visited their routine was the same. The smallest park would take between one or two hours to traverse because they meandered along pathways, stopping to admire roses, watch birds, read inscriptions or smile at babies. Doris ever alert to Robert and his pain would suggest that they sat down for a few minutes to catch their breath. Robert always agreed, though he never made the suggestion.

If there was a cafe in the park, they would have a light lunch or tea and a scone. Occasionally they decided beforehand to bring a picnic. Doris made tuna or salmon sandwiches, brought slices of her homemade cake and a flask of tea. Robert carried fried chicken, salad, fresh fruit and a carton of juice along with paper plates, napkins, plastic knives and forks and cups. Sometimes they sat opposite each other seated at a wooden picnic table, the meal laid out between them. At other times they sat side by side on a bench with the food filling a small space in the middle.

They walked and they talked. They sat and they looked around, above and beyond. They talked. Sometimes they just sat as they did now, in a silence that cut them off from the noise of traffic, barking dogs or screaming children. A silence that enveloped them, brought them together without the need to say anything. Doris, never having felt like this before, pondered whether this was love, if love felt like this. Whatever it was, in fact, it was different from what she had felt for Frank. 'Perhaps', she mumbled, 'it is because I can't remember. It was all so long ago.'

'Yu was saying?'

'What was I saying? Oh yes, this rose garden is lovely isn't it?'

And to herself, 'You silly thing why didn't you tell him what you were thinking?'

Later, they walked slowly up the steep hill towards the bandstand. By the time they arrived, they were both of them panting and out of breath. A sheen of perspiration lay on Robert's forehead. He mopped at it with his handkerchief. Her face was pink with the exertion. A trickle of sweat ran down the centre of her spine.

'Thank goodness there is somewhere to sit,' she murmured, sinking down onto the carved, graffiti-covered seat. Robert said nothing as he carefully lowered himself down beside her.

A clear panorama lay spread before them: Battersea power station to the left, Canary Wharf to the right. Sounds of traffic floated up to them while behind them in a tree, a squirrel chattered angrily.

'We have covered a lot of ground these past few months, haven't we?'

Doris broke the silence.

'Yes, an we still have plenty more places to go. Yu like comin out wid me, Doris?'

A pause.

'Yes, yes, I do.'

She patted his hand, then let hers lie resting on top of his.

'We been doin dis for about a year now, yu know.'

'Is it really as long as that?'

'Who woulda thought that losin mi way woulda led to meetin yu.'

'I always sleep like a log when I get home after a day out with you.'

'Mi too.'

'I sleep well, but I have dreams, too,' she mused. Her family would be outraged if they knew of her dreams. There was no way she could possibly go on a trip and not return the same day without telling them. A daytrip extending to a weekend away, or staying overnight in a hotel. Single or a double room? Now that was something else. Her thoughts strayed further. She and Robert spending the night together. In the same room. In the same bed!

Never. Yet there was always the possibility. 'I wonder what it would be like?' She stopped herself. It was ridiculous, someone of her age having these thoughts. But she was and she did and she had before. Dreamt about it. Tried to imagine what it might be like.

Of course she'd only ever known Frank. Was that sex or making love? Anyway, it was not likely to ever happen because Robert was too much of a gentleman to suggest such a thing. But was she too much of a lady? A small cloud drifted across the sky, briefly obliterating the sun. She shivered, moved closer to him and pushed the outrageous thoughts to the back of her mind.

8

Sitting in the De La Warr pavilion at Bexhill on Sea, listening to a brass band playing a medley of film signature tunes, Doris glanced at Robert. She'd been sneaking little glances at him all day. Each time her eyes caught his, they smiled at each other. When he appeared unaware of her eyes watching him, she let her gaze linger. On his closely cropped greying hair. His curly salt and pepper eyebrows. His wide nose, set between those gentle brown eyes. His lips, how they felt, that first kiss in Richmond park, the day he gave her the mango. There had been a lot of firsts recently. And now here they were on their first real day trip. A trip to the coast.

She had suggested the day out, following several weeks of warm sunny weather that was forecast not to break for a while. They were returning from a visit to a large park on the outskirts of Bromley where a country fair had been in progress for several days. It always surprised her that they never bumped into anyone she knew. London was a large place, yes, but her friends and acquaintances were always talking about the different places they visited during the week, when they were not at the lunch club. The venues were similar to those she and Robert visited occasionally.

'Shall we go on a trip to the coast one day?'

She sat with her hat in her lap on the inside of the seat next to the window as the bus moved slowly up the hill towards the town. Her bare arm touched his.

'If this weather holds out for a little while longer and before the school summer holidays, we could go by train. What do you think, dear?' Now's your chance, Doris. Suggest making it a weekend, she thought. Too late, the moment was gone.

'Where do you want to go?' He turned towards her.

'Well, Bexhill on Sea would be nice. I have been there with my club a couple of times. It is a quiet place, not full of arcades and rides or that sort of thing. You don't get many young people there.'

'And if it rain while we down there?'

She told him of the pavilion. How they often have live bands playing music. They could always sit in there if the weather broke, but she didn't think it would. 'The weatherman says it is good for a while yet.'

'Then we'll go next week?'

The remainder of the journey was spent making plans.

'We can have fish and chips for lunch while we are there. That way we won't have too much to carry.'

'What about swimming?'

'Well, I don't think it will be warm enough yet, but it may be okay to get our feet wet so perhaps a small towel. Do you know how to get there?'

Was it really her taking charge, making all of the arrangements? A new Doris, more confident, assertive, was emerging and he didn't seem to object. All the years of being directed where to go, told what to do, and in some cases how to do it. First Frank, then her children, especially bossy Joan. They would be surprised. She always checked with Robert if he minded, if it was alright with him. Not like the family who informed her of their decisions without including her in the discussion. Or they made suggestions that brooked no argument anyway.

Robert, after years of having to make decisions for himself, quite welcomed being asked his opinion and having someone else take over. Besides, he liked Doris, enjoyed being with her, couldn't imagine what his weekly outing would have been like without her. He wasn't even sure if he would have kept them up.

They met at the station at ten o'clock. Their first big trip together. An adventure for both of them. Doris wore a wide brimmed straw hat, purchased for her by her daughter when she accompanied the family on their annual holiday to Teneriffe, as the unofficial baby sitter, of course.

'You must have something to keep the sun off your head and neck while you are on the beach with the children, mum.'

Making a decision about what to wear was difficult. Skirt and blouse, trousers and shirt. Eventually she decided to wear the dress she wore the day they met, with a white hand knitted cardigan and white sandals. In her bag was a fold-up plastic raincoat, a small towel and some suncream, just in case they did sit on the beach. Robert wore a pair of stone coloured trousers, a green and brown check shirt and a light brown flat cap. His jacket was over his arm. He carried a small back pack and, of course, his walking stick. Renting two deckchairs they carefully made their way across the pebbles to a strip of sand and sat facing the sea, watching seagulls wheel and dip into the white crested waves.

A familiar peacefulness surrounded them. It felt comforting and comfortable. Robert reached inside his jacket pocket and offered Doris a mint. She took it, murmuring her thanks. Resuming her position she wondered what he was thinking about.

'Are you hungry?'

'No, not really. De tea and bun we ate on de train is fine for de present.'

'Tell me when you are ready for lunch and we will go to the fish and chip shop. Alright?'

About a half an hour later as the sun settled overhead, she pulled her bag from beneath the chair and rummaged for her sun cream. She began to massage it into each arm, moving her hands in a circular motion towards her shoulders. Arms crossed, she struggled to reach the back of her shoulders. Joan or Billy usually did it for her when they were away together.

'Here, let me.'

Taking the plastic bottle from her where it lay in her lap, he squeezed the white cream into the palm of his hands and rubbed them together. Then leaning over from his chair, he placed a hand on each of her shoulders and began to smooth it onto her skin. Doris closed her eyes. Kisses were one thing. But this! She felt his warm breath on the side of her neck, or was it the breeze. It had been a long time. Oh, that felt good.

'How's that?'

'Fine. Fine, thank you. Thank you.'

Doris suggested paddling in the sea.

'I never been in de sea before.'

'What? But you come from Jamaica. How come you have never been in the sea. You can swim.'

'Remember I tole you dat I learn to swim in de river. In Jamaica I live in de country, long way from de coast. When mi was a likkle bwoy we didnt have no motor car. My daddy him did have a bicycle an most people in dem days, dem did only have a donkey. Not even de bus did come to where we live. We did have to walk a long, long way down to de road where de bus did stop to ketch it.'

She leant forward, 'Pardon?'

There were occasions when Robert was talking to her, when she didn't understand what he was saying. During the eighteen months of meeting with him, Doris had grown used to his habit of using Jamaican patois from time to time. Some months earlier she realised that until they met, she had thought that Jamaicans, like Africans, spoke a completely foreign language. Then she began to listen more intently to the voices she heard when travelling on buses or in the supermarket queue. She found that she was soon able to differentiate between language and accent. Now she accepted that Robert felt so comfortable with her that he probably didn't realise that he was using his patois anyway. She also recognised that when Billy and his friend visited on Saturday mornings to run errands for her, his conversations with his friend was interspersed with cockney Jamaican.

Robert repeated himself and added, 'The first time me did see the sea, I was about twelve years old. Mi daddy him took me to Portland where him did have a job to do. But mi still never went in de sea.'

'But I thought it was only a small island.'

'Yes, small in comparison to England but it still big. England is an island, too, an me sure dat dere is people who never yet been to de seaside.'

'I suppose so.'

'Wont de water be cold?'

'It may be. But once you've walked in it for a while it begins to feel warm.'

She bent forward and removed her sandals, pleased she hadn't worn tights that might have proved difficult to remove. Standing, she waited for him to take off his socks and shoes. She watched as he rolled his socks neatly, before placing them inside his shoes. Gingerly, they walked over the stones towards the breaking waves. Doris was first to get her feet wet. Lifting her skirt to her thighs she edged forward. She turned then and called, 'Come on, it isn't too bad.'

Robert bent and rolled up his trouser legs to his knees. His stick was way behind him with their other belongings on the deckchairs. He felt vulnerable, apprehensive as he painstakingly moved towards her outstretched hand.

The cold water swept in and over his feet. He gasped and staggered backwards, almost losing his balance. Doris grabbed his arm, steadied him and waited. Then she took his hand.

'Come on, stand with me, here. There are no stones just here. That's right, better now?'

The water still felt cold, rushing in, splashing his shins, curling around his calves before receding with a soft sshh, then gathering momentum to engulf his feet again. Gradually the pounding in his chest slowed, his grip on her hand relaxed, the tension in his back subsided and he began to enjoy the sensation of the water around his toes. Doris felt him relaxing and smiled at him.

'There, I told you. Feels good?'

He nodded. 'It doesn't feel cold now either.'

Shading his eyes, the deckchair attendant watched them from his windbreak against the wall. First time he had ever seen a mixed race couple together, well, an old couple, pensioners they must be. They were standing side by side with their backs to him. Knee deep in the water, holding hands. He saw the woman reach out with her other hand and turning, touch the old man's face. Perhaps she was brushing something from his cheek. Then the old man turned. They were facing each other, they moved closer. It was like watching a film, he thought. Two people, an almost cloudless June sky, the sun directly above them so there were no shadows. Tenderly they leant towards each other and kissed.

'It wasn't a long passionate kiss or anything like that,' he was to tell his girlfriend later. 'More like from where I could see, as if their lips were brushing together.'

'Then?'

'Then what?'

'What happened next, stupid?'

'Oh then they just stood there side by side again holding hands. Watching the sea I suppose.'

'I wonder what it felt like?'

'What felt like?'

'Kissing a black man and an old black man at that.'

The fish and chip lunch was delicious. They had decided to carry their meal back across the road and sit in a shelter on the front to eat. People passed in front and behind the small three-sided metal structure. Some glanced in at the couple sitting close to each other on the wooden bench. One or two looked a second time. Most just carried on walking. Robert put his arm around her shoulders and she leaned into him, closing her eyes, inhaling his aftershave mingled with the tangy vinegary scent of salt and chips. She felt his head against hers.

They must have dozed off, and woke simultaneously to the raucous screech of two gulls fighting over a piece of bread. Doris looked at her watch.

'Let's go up to the pavilion and listen to the band for a while.'

The pavilion, once a proud architectural structure, was badly in need of renovation. Nevertheless, there was a small crowd of mainly elderly people sitting at the tables drinking tea and nodding in time to the music. After finding a vacant table near the back against the glass wall, Doris left Robert to go and purchase a cup of tea for both of them.

An hour passed listening to familiar tunes, watching people, glancing at each other, smiling with their eyes, averting them shyly, looking back again. Until it was time to walk back to the station, the waiting train, home.

Leaning against each other as the train travelled towards London, they scarcely spoke. They were the only occupants, suspended in a moving capsule, wrapped, cocoon-like in a soft aura of well being, comfortable, his head resting once more lightly on hers, their hands intertwined in her lap. And then Doris began to giggle. It welled up from her stomach to her chest and bubbled through her lips as her shoulders began to quiver, silently at first, then because she couldn't control it any longer, mischievously bursting out from her. She lifted his hand with hers and pressed it against her lips to try and still the eruption. Tears of laughter began to well in her eyes and tumble down her reddening cheeks.

'Oh dear, oh dear, oh dear.'

Robert, puzzled though relieved that she wasn't upset, watched, waiting for her to calm down and explain what she found so hilarious.

'It's alright, Robert. I was just thinking what a wonderful day this has been. Don't you think so?'

Doris took the proffered tissue and dabbed her eyes. She hiccupped like a baby. Robert looked confused.

'Yes', he affirmed, 'the day was wonderful. Not funny, but wonderful. So why the hysterical laughing?'

On the last lap of her homeward journey, after bidding Robert goodbye, Doris was overcome with the giggles again. No-one on the bus noticed the grey-haired woman in a white cardigan with a straw hat perched at a rakish angle on her head laughing to herself. Laughing because she was trying to imagine what her daughter and sons would have thought if they could have seen her holding hands while paddling in the sea with Robert. If other passengers did notice her, then they probably assumed that she was mad or drunk. Doris felt both.

9

Just across the river from Greenwich is a tiny park called Jubilee Gardens. It isn't really a park at all, but a strip of green with ancient plane trees running along the side of the Thames. There is a tea room there, a newspaper kiosk and a few benches.

Robert and Doris walked slowly past the Cutty Sark sailing ship one afternoon, across the cobbled open space and entered the lift that carried travellers down to the tunnel which ran south to north below the river.

Young children, apparently on a school journey, ran screaming past them, their excited voices echoing back off the low ceiling and rolling to meet Doris and Robert, who slowed almost to a standstill as they hurtled past.

Tourists with video cameras and backpacks overtook them and disappeared into the waiting lift which rose upwards, then returned to disgorge more subterranean walkers. Emerging blinking into the bright sunlight, they both paused to gain their bearings before turning right into the gardens. A flock of pigeons rose with a flurry of wings, scattering seed, crumbs and dust in the dry air. Everywhere there seemed to be a film of dust. The air was very still. During the three weeks since their day at Bexhill, rain had only fallen twice during the night. Doris wore her straw hat. Her sleeveless cotton dress revealed tanned freckled shoulders. Robert also wore a cap though today he had left his jacket at home.

'Let's sit by de river', he said. 'We might get a likkle breeze dere.'

'Would you like a drink first?'

Doris, ever mindful of his hip condition changed her question to, 'You go over to that bench there, where the tree overhangs it and makes it shady and I'll bring us a drink. Do you want tea or something cold?'

'I feel sure there'll be a thunderstorm soon,' she commented on her return to his side. 'There you are, a nice cold drink of fruit juice, and an ice cream. It is vanilla you like isn't it?'

'Yu is gettin to know me real well, Doris. Tank-you.'

A smile spread across her lightly suntanned cheeks. She made herself comfortable beside him and sipped her tea.

Across the river on the Greenwich side they could see people queuing to embark in readiness for a trip to Westminster. Apart from a couple of men sitting at one of the tables near the cafe, they were the only people in the park. The pigeons had returned and were busily pecking around the table and chair legs. Doris sighed. On Saturday she and her family were going to Teneriffe for ten days. Joan, her daughter, had as usual booked it before telling Doris of the arrangements. She always assumes that I want to be with them, thought Doris.

'What's de matter?'

'Is it that obvious?'

'Well de way dat you sighed jus now mek me tink.'

'Don't get me wrong, Robert, I love my family. But sometimes they can be, well, a bit too much.'

'What yu mean?'

Explaining to him what Joan had done she added,

'It's not that I don't want to go on holiday with them. It's that they never ask me first. Besides, it also means that I will miss two Wednesdays with you. What about your children? Are they like that with you?'

'No. No. Me does tink sometime dat I did brung dem up to be too independent. Dey look after me, yes, but dey does know dat I am very independent and dont need dem like you need your family.'

'But that's the whole point Robert, dear. They don't give me a chance. If they just asked me first, allowed me to refuse.'

'Well we jus do tings differently, eh.'

'I never did get to meet your children after that Sunday, when I was coming to have dinner with you and Billie went down with his appendix.'

'I remember. Was a good ting dat we made de arrangement to meet every Wednesday at de cafe wasn't it?'

'Yes, otherwise we might not still be seeing each other.'

'I thank de lord for dat.'

'Are you a Christian, Robert?'

'Well, me dont really go to no church hexceptin for special occasions or when sister Priscilla come drag me out of the house.'

'Sister Priscilla, who's she?'

'She de mos determined woman me did ever know after mi children's mother. My children dey always laugh at me and her cos dey tink dat she got her sights on marrying me.'

Doris's heart lurched.

'And will you?'

'Will I what?'

'Marry her, of course.'

'No, no, me not gonna marry anybody. Sister Priscilla can chase me an chase me long as she like. I ain't never had another woman after de children's mother lef me.'

'Oh my dear.'

It was funny how her heart seemed to settle after he said that. Robert didn't seem inclined to elaborate any further but added that he still wanted her to meet his children and perhaps they could arrange another date after her holiday.

'The only people who have a holiday when we go away are my grown up children,' she remarked grimly. All I get is a change of scenery and to watch the little ones who would probably be happier in their paddling pools in their back gardens or at the local swimming pool.'

In the distance they heard a low growl of thunder. The sun beat down on the glistening river which washed against the embankment with a gentle swish, reminding them both of their seaside trip.

'Families are funny things you know,' she sighed.

'Well, you can come an' judge mine against yours one day soon.'

Robert reflected on the past year and the change in his life style since retirement. Never in his wildest dreams, and he didn't have many of them, did he think that he would have a companion with him on his travels. If only his damn leg didn't trouble him so. He liked Doris. In fact, he admitted to himself, he was fond of her. He recalled the kiss in Richmond Park. Who made that first move? Whenever he cut into the orange flesh of a mango he was assailed with the scent and memory of their first kiss. On the trip to the coast, knee deep in the water, holding hands they kissed again. And in between when they said goodbye each week they briefly brushed each other's cheeks as friends do when meeting or parting.

She often held his hand now, too, touching or patting him spontaneously, leaning into him and letting him lean against her. He loved the faint lavender smell that wafted from her when she was close to him, the way her hair curled at the nape of her neck, the way she sometimes called him 'dear'. Was he, he wondered falling in love? Even if he was, he wasn't sure how to show her, tell her, let her know the depth of his growing feelings for her. A sudden breeze caused a flurry of dry leaves and discarded cartons to swirl along the path. Again the thunder sounded, louder, nearer, more ominous. Small white clouds appeared in the sky.

'Sounds like the weather is going to break.' Her tone was apologetic.

'Yu tink we should start headin back?'

'Yes, dear. Let me put these things in the bin first.'

Even in the daylight the brilliance of the lightening flash was visible. It was followed by a ground-shaking roll of thunder. Robert felt a tingle run up his spine. She'd called him 'dear' again.

While Doris went on holiday with her family, Robert tended his garden. He shopped locally. He visited the pensioners' club and played dominoes with his contemporaries. He didn't visit a park for the two weeks that Doris was away. He missed her.

When they met in the cafe following her return, he told her, 'I didn't feel like going on mi own, not widout yu to talk to.'

'I thought about you, too, and wondered what you were doing, especially on Wednesdays. Now where shall we go today? Have you got your little book with you?'

August and September brought changeable weather and although they continued with their weekly outings, Robert and Doris were often forced to sit in cafes or take refuge beneath large trees or bandstands within the parks. They tried to restrict their journeys to suburban parks, travelling around the outskirts of the city, avoiding central London buses that were filled with visiting tourists and parents taking their bored offspring to visit museums or exhibitions.

Both of them returned to their respective homes, tired and weary though always looking forward to the following week and being together again. Doris, seated at her kitchen table, a mug of steaming tea in front of her, recalled her day. Retracing minute details, going over conversations, reliving holding Robert's hand, his touch, his lips brushing her cheek. And later alone in her bed she slept soundly before dreaming.

Robert was always overcome with exhaustion by the time he reached his garden gate. Pausing to regain his breath, straighten up and feel for his door key, he would mutter to himself, rub his aching hip and make his way painfully along the path to his front door. Inside, he often took a full fifteen to twenty minutes to recover from the walk to his home from the bus stop. Sitting on the stool that stood in the hallway next to the coat stand, he took great gulps of air. One hand rested on his knee, the other covered his eyes. Gradually, the furious pounding of his heart slowed, the ragged breaths became less laboured and the knife-like pain subsided. Then he would move slowly and carefully down the hall into his kitchen where, after pouring himself a drink of rum he'd sit in his armchair and evaluate the day. He, too, would sleep soundly, aided by the painkillers and the day's exertions.

Unlike the previous year when an Indian summer heralded a late autumn, October arrived with cold misty mornings followed by grey days of drizzle.

'I feel as if it has been raining since we came back from our holiday,' Doris remarked one afternoon as once again they were forced to take shelter. 'Let's go swimming next week. We'll get wet but at least it will be comfortable.'

'From now on, Doris, we have to plan some indoor adventures for de both of us, eh?'

10

The day Doris won the tea dance tickets in a raffle held at her lunch club, their meetings changed. The tickets could be used at one of three different venues in South East London. Doris was relieved at that because when she'd been announced as the winner, her friend Amy suggested that she accompany her. Amy was visibly hurt when Doris didn't agree with her about going together and having a 'bit of fun,' as she put it.

'We could be like those ladies that Joyce Grenfell sings about in that song, 'Stately as a Galleon.'

Doris agreed with that. Amy was tall and statuesque with a large firm bosom. Doris herself was plump though equally proportioned and the vision of herself clasped to Amy's bosom gliding across the dance floor at Brixton Town Hall made her smile.

'I have a friend I would like to take with me,' she said, shaking her head at Amy's request. Amy was curious as to who Doris could possibly want to go dancing with. After all, she and Doris moved in the same circles and knew each other's friends. They had been going to the lunch club twice a week for several years now. Both of them were widows welcoming the daytime companionship which the local authority social club offered.

Along with other women and some men of similar ages they gathered for a nourishing, reasonably priced meal, a game of bingo, with practical prizes and some light gossip. The club also ran theatre trips, coach outings and low season holidays. Several Autumn romances had blossomed in the club and there had been at least three weddings in as many years. The most surprising of all was the one between Emily Jones, a spinster of seventy-five and Albert Palmer, a widower of sixty-nine. Emily had worn a white suit with a cocky little hat and veil. 'Seventy-five years old and still a virgin,' Amy whispered as she and Doris stood together watching the newly married couple walk down the aisle. A year later, on their first anniversary, Amy, with her raucous laugh and stock of ever-so-slightly risque jokes pondered on whether Emily was still in the same state.

Until Doris began going out with Robert, she had never questioned that all the patrons at her club were white. No Indians, no black people either. She wondered if any ever tried to join. Perhaps they wouldn't care for the food, she thought, as she and Robert sat together on one of their picnics and she savoured the chicken drumstick and fried dumpling he had brought. She knew that he went to a similar club in Lewisham and that most of the patrons were of Caribbean origin. The few white people who attended were husbands or wives or had once been. Now Doris found herself trying to explain to Amy that this friend was one that Amy had not met and no the friend did not live locally. The last hour at the club was a little frosty with Amy acting rather foolishly, Doris thought.

Anyway, she and Robert made arrangements to meet early in Lewisham, have a light lunch in one of the cafes and then travel on to Woolwich town hall where tea dances were held every Wednesday afternoon. Robert had laughed when Doris told him of her prize and suggested that they go together. He had also made excuses about his hip. But he added,

'I used to be a good dancer when me was a young man. You should have seen me in me zoot suit and me hat and me two-tone shoes. Man I could move in dem days. Champion I was, den.'

He chuckled to himself as he recollected arriving at the local dance hall in Crofts Hill, Jamaica, shoes caked in red mud, but trouser bottoms clean and still sharply creased having been carefully rolled up to the knees for the walk from Corner where he lived. The music thumped out the beat of the latest Ska song while he cleaned his shoes before entering the darkened hall already heaving with bodies.

'Well you won't have to move too much at this dance,' Doris had smiled. 'We could try a waltz or two. I don't think that will affect your leg. And anyway, if it does, it will be nice to sit and watch, won't it?'

She noticed that he had swallowed two white pills with his lunch. They were, he told her, painkillers. If he took them regularly, then he hardly felt the grinding pain. He hoped that it wouldn't be too long now before his operation and then he would really show her how to dance.

At the Town Hall, Doris produced the tickets. She was given a bunch of roses and congratulated on being the lucky winner for that month. They were led to a small table for two where a pot of tea and biscuits had been left. The trio of musicians looked as if they were members of an old people's club. But the music they were playing was pleasant and inviting.

Doris and Robert sat and watched as assorted couples moved across the shining wooden floor. There were men dancing with women and twirling each other, feet moving exactly in time to the music. There were women dancing with each other as precisely as the mixed couples. There were also couples who were not taking the outing quite so seriously and were laughing and giggling as they tripped, caught each other's toes or missed the outstretched hand on a turn. There was one black couple moving like experts. Backs straight, heads thrown back, arms outstretched, they executed a perfect tango. Robert and Doris were the only couple of mixed race. She looked at him across the table, at his greying hair, his smoothly-shaven cheeks and the little hairline moustache above his lips. The lips that she had first kissed that afternoon in Richmond Park just over a year ago. Had she really? Yes, in a place as public as this dance hall, except that then they were the only people there. And the dancers had been the autumn leaves. She reached across the table and took his hand, 'If you won't ask me to dance, then I will have to ask you, won't I?'

Walking to the edge of the dance floor, Robert slipped his arm around her waist. Doris lifted her arm to encircle his shoulders.

Her other hand found his. For an instant they paused, waiting for the right moment to join in the movement, and then they were dancing. The tune was 'Tea for Two.' Robert was humming it as he held her close. She could smell his aftershave each time her face brushed against his corded jacket. She wondered if he could smell her perfume. They danced, weaving in and out of the other dancers, both of them singing now like most of the other couples. When the dance was over they remained standing close together, still holding hands, waiting for the next tune. A waltz this time. A familiar tune but the title evaded her. She closed her eyes and let Robert guide her. He held her, afraid that she would be offended if his arm was too tight around her waist. All too soon, the waltz ended and they drifted back to their seats where the tea pot had been replenished.

Sitting in silence sipping tea, Doris's foot tapped lightly in time to the cha cha cha. She was aware of Robert's fingers drumming the rhythm on the pink spotted cloth covering the table. Once again the trio struck up a waltz. This time Doris knew the words. 'Silver Threads Among The Gold.' Looking at each other, and with no need to ask, she stood, moved into his already open arms and as they stepped onto the floor marvelled at herself.

Never in all her life could she have imagined herself dancing with a black person. She didn't think that she was prejudiced, though she knew that both she and Frank would never have consented to any of their children marrying one. She always acknowledged her eldest grandson's friend and even let him bring him into her house when he came to run errands on Saturday mornings. She gave him lunch and pocket money when he did little jobs for her while he was there. She spoke to the children in the doctor's surgery when, as toddlers do, a little hand would be placed on her knee and a child would say trustingly, 'Hello.'

Frank had occasionally passed disparaging comments about the man who ran the local chemist and his brother in the post office. Yet he discussed cricket scores and performances with them, compared player against player and agreed when England gave a poor performance. He stubbornly refused to eat anything other than English food, his reason being that he had tasted enough foreign stuff when he was in the army, stationed in Malaya and later stationed in Malta. It crossed her mind that if he could see her from whereever he was now, he would probably die all over again of shock.

She drew closer to Robert and closed her eyes. Encircled by his arms, Doris pushed away the thoughts of her late husband, refusing to allow any feelings of disquiet about her family to spoil the moment. She was disappointed when the next dance began turning out to be too fast for Robert to dance comfortably. Doris glanced down at her hand lying on the cloth. She still wore her wedding ring, a plain band of gold. Nothing fancy. Over forty years on the same finger. It was a part of her now. Worn a little thin underneath but still there symbolizing the foreverness of marriage. The vows were: 'Until death do you part.' Death had certainly parted her and Frank. Yet she still wore the ring. Perhaps the other dancers thought that she and Robert were married. Now that would be something if she were.

A little while later the leader of the trio asked if there were any anniversaries or birthdays being celebrated. The next few minutes passed singing 'Happy Birthday' to various people. Then the 'Anniversary Waltz' began.

'I'm sure all of you here can think of something to celebrate today,' said the leader.

Almost every one was on the floor. Hardly a chair was occupied. All the dancers including Robert and Doris were singing. The large silver ball overhead turned casting stars across the floor and upon them. When the music ceased, the clapping began and continued until the musicians struck up again. Doris wanted to ask Robert if there was any reason why today was special to him but changed her mind as they began to dance. Today will always be special to me, she thought. This is the closest I have been to a man since Frank died.

Dancing close to Robert felt good; would being married to him feel the same? 'Now stop this Doris,' she told herself sharply. And she inhaled again the scent of his aftershave. One more dance, then the familiar strains of 'Last Waltz.' She didn't sing this time but leant against him totally relaxed.

Emerging from the town hall to a cold drizzle that soon turned to steady rain, Doris clutched her roses in one hand and held Robert's arm with the other. It wasn't far to the bus stop but she could tell he was having difficulty walking.

'Will you be all right?'

She looked at him with concern. 'We could get a taxi if you want to.'

Shaking his head and straightening his shoulders, he refused the offer.

'I'll be fine once we get on the bus.'

They stood close together, heads bent against the rain and discussed the music and the merits of the trio. The weather looked suspiciously as if it was about to call a temporary halt to their weekly outings. Doris did not want to give up meeting Robert but apart from swimming or these tea dances, she couldn't think of anywhere suitable. Neither did she want to share Robert with her friends. Not yet, anyway. There were museums they could visit but she wasn't sure if entrance for pensioners was free or not.

'You could come to my house one day if you like,' said Robert.

Before she could answer him, Doris saw a bus turn the corner. She put out her hand to hail it.

The bus was almost full with only a few single seats empty. They travelled without being able to talk to each other. Doris stood in the aisle a short way down from Robert who after struggling up the lurching vehicle managed to squeeze onto the long seat at the rear.

In Lewisham the bus filled quickly. Doris stood. She flatly refused the offer of his seat, insisting that he needed it more than she did. In no time at all the bus arrived at Stondon Park where Robert, grimacing as he pulled himself upright, waved goodbye to Doris who was by now sitting in his seat. Through the window she could see him as he walked, head down into the rain, leg dragging slightly towards the road leading to his house. He had tried to assure Doris that the outing had been most enjoyable. It was just his leg that didn't agree. Doris imagined she heard the sharp intake of breath when he hoisted himself onto his feet. Nevertheless, he had smiled and waved before pushing past the other passengers.

Rubbing the steamy glass she tapped the window but he didn't hear. 'We haven't made any arrangements for next week,' she mouthed through the glass. Robert limped on. Doris tapped again to no avail. She leaned back on the seat hearing once more the music to which they had danced that afternoon. Humming to herself the elusive words of the familiar tune came to her. Eyes closed as she recalled Robert's arms and the smell of his aftershave, she sung, 'Que Sera Sera, Whatever will be, will be.'

11

Robert paused before he opened the gate to his home. His body was suffused by a terrible burning pain that gripped his hip, leg and back. Briefly he wondered if he would make it down the path to the front door. Grasping the cold, wet metal gate he gritted his teeth and pushed it open. When he lifted his right foot, the intense pain took his breath away. Grunting out loud he placed his other hand on the top bar to steady himself before attempting to take another step.

Although it was only a matter of minutes before he reached the front door, it seemed to take hours. Despite the rain and the cold wind, by the time he pushed his key into the lock he was bathed in perspiration. There was a red mist before his eyes and his heart was beating so hard, he thought that it would burst through his skin. Closing the door behind him, he leant heavily against it until the pain subsided a little before attempting to cross the hallway. In the darkness he shuffled to his room and fell into a chair.

His breath came now in rasping, short, sharp bursts that hurt almost as much as his leg. The beating of his heart resonated in his ears. Fumbling in his pocket he pulled out a cotton handkerchief and wiped away the rain and sweat that was cooling on his forehead and face.

The action seemed to calm him and slowly his breathing eased, becoming more regular as he forced himself to take deep breaths.

'Jesus Lord,' he heard himself say out loud. 'If dis is what dancing does to me, den dere is no way me an mistress Doris is goin again, free tickets or not.'

His hand froze in midair when he realized they'd parted without arranging where they would go. Before he could begin to get his head around what to do next, he heard the front door opening and his daughter's voice calling, 'Anyone at home?'

Sharon's greeting was always the same even when it was obvious he was there. The light came on blinding him momentarily.

'Daddy what are you doing sitting here in the dark? I didn't think you were home. Why are you in the dark anyway? Has something happened to you? Did you know that the key was still in the lock? Daddy, are you okay?'

Her questions tumbled out leaving no space for him to reply. She crossed the room and knelt down beside the chair as he struggled to get up. The movement caused the pain to return and an involuntary groan escaped his lips. He gripped the sides of the chair and tried again to rise. The red mist descended once more forcing him to take deep breaths to prevent himself from crying out loud.

'Daddy, what's wrong?' Sharon held his hand.

He was waiting until the pain subsided before replying. But he saw the consternation in her face, heard the panic in her voice.

'Is it your heart? Where's the pain? Shall I call the doctor?'

Never having seen her father like this, her anxiety increased with every second he took to respond. His eyes were closed, he was inhaling long, slow breaths through his teeth, whistling with each exhalation. Beads of sweat glistened on his forehead. His hands gripped the arms of the chair, fingers deep in the upholstery. He held up one finger and finally managed to gasp.

'Wait.'

He began to breathe normally. His grip on the chair relaxed. Drained and weak, he fumbled in his lap for the handkerchief. He mopped his face and brow again.

'Jus a likkle pain in mi foot.' He managed a weak smile. 'Is alright now.' Patting her hand he continued,

'Ah went dancin wid mi friend today an it jus mek mi foot hurt a likkle bit.'

He made no attempt to rise from the chair.

'But daddy, your key was still in the door. How long have you been sitting here in the dark?'

'Me jus come in.'

He ignored the question about the key. He did not want to believe he could have been so careless.

'Mek me a drink now, chile.'

Sharon stood up. She removed the tailored jacket that matched the pinstriped trousers she was wearing, shook her long locks free and hung the jacket on the back of a chair. She spoke to her father again.

'Let me put the kettle on. Then I want you to tell me what really is wrong. You gave me such a scare just now.' She left the room and while she was gone his thoughts returned once more to Doris and his tardiness at not finalising the venue of their next outing. How was he going to contact her?

Every week prior to parting, they had planned what they would do or where they would go the following week even though they always met first in the cafe on the Parade. He recognised that the distraction of the throbbing pain in his leg, the extreme fatigue of the homeward journey, plus the fact that he had been sitting apart from Doris, were the reasons they had made no plans. If they had been able to sit together on the bus, they would have made some sort of arrangements. When the bus finally drew up at his stop, getting up and off had taken every ounce of effort and concentration. There was hardly enough energy to wave goodbye to her.

He was interrupted by the appearance of Sharon carrying two steaming mugs.

'Why dey not on a tray? Didn't I always tell yu it safer on a tray?'

She ignored the questions and placed the red mug with 'Dad' written in bold black letters on it beside him on the small table. She did remember to place a coaster beneath the mug, knowing that not to do so would bring forth another question and a reminder of her childhood.

She was concerned about her father who never complained about his health. Come to think of it, he was never ill. There was this little problem with his leg. Although he regularly attended the doctor to get a prescription for pain killers, there was never any indication of the severity of the pain. An appointment with an orthopaedic surgeon confirmed the GP's diagnosis of an arthritic hip and told him it was not ripe enough for surgery. When it was, he would be put on the waiting list. This might take between two and four years before he would get a replacement. Meanwhile, his task, according to the surgeon, was to try and keep as mobile as possible. Go swimming or go home to the sunshine. Robert's indignation at the final comment caused him to tell his children.

'Who im tink he is? Tellin me to go back 'ome. Jus so im ave one less patient to hoperate on.' They had all laughed at the way his anger caused him to revert to Jamaican patois.

'Well, I aint goin nowhere. I been here dis long an me pay mi stamp an all. An me entikle to an hoperation ifn me haf to wait forhever, God forbid!'

Nevertheless, though he rarely complained he had only in the past eighteen months or so begun to use the stick that stood in the corner beside the front door.

'Jus cos mi have a bad foot dont mean mi an old man,' he had grumbled one day when his youngest son suggested he use it. He still pottered about in the garden, though a couple of times he had asked very reluctantly for help when he couldn't manage to use the spade or fork to wrest a clump of plants from the earth. And he still insisted on cooking for the whole family most Sundays and public holidays.

'Daddy.'

She sat down opposite him and spoke softly. 'When I came in just now you really scared me. I thought you were having a heart attack or something. Please tell me what is the matter with you.'

'Aint nuttin the matter wid me.'

Lifting the still steaming mug, he took a sip. He needed a painkiller now and time to let its effects take over before he could get up from the chair.

'Of course there is something wrong and if you won't tell me, I will have to call the boys and your doctor to come and sort you out. Oh you are so stubborn.'

Robert sipped again. He felt in his coat pocket for the plastic bottle of pills. 'I know that something is wrong because you still have your coat on. And you would never leave the key in the door. Come on, daddy, let me help you get that wet coat off.' She rose and moved toward him.

'Dont need any help,' he muttered trying to lift himself from the chair.

'Aagh!' He fell back as fire coursed down his leg. He felt tears well up in his eyes and quickly covered them lest Sharon see.

'Daddy.' She knelt beside him. 'Please tell me. What is it?'

He continued to stubbornly deny the cause while allowing her to help him remove the damp coat and take the bottle from the pocket.

Realizing that the cause of the pain was his leg, Sharon felt more in control.

'How long will it take for these to begin to have any effect?'

'About half an hour.' Robert's voice was husky with pain and tiredness.

'Listen, dad, I'm going to call the doctor to see if he can prescribe anything stronger and get your appointment for the surgeon brought forward.'

'No, dont trouble dem. Dey busy enough. She caan do nuttin. I have to wait mi turn, wait for mi name to move up di list.'

'Not if I have anything to do with it.'

Sharon stood and left the room taking her mobile telephone with her. Robert tried hard to listen but her voice in the kitchen was indistinct and he was feeling exhausted. He drifted off to sleep, the half drunk mug of tea beside him. He was awoken by the doorbell ringing. Before he could attempt to rise, he heard Sharon's voice.

'I'll get it, dad.'

Robert looked at the clock. It was almost seven thirty. Late for him. Time he should be washing up the dishes from his evening meal. But he hadn't eaten. Carefully placing his hands on either side of the arm chair, he tried to lift himself upwards. Testing, he placed his good leg firmly on the carpet. As he tried to put his weight on the floor, Sharon entered with the doctor. She was apologizing for calling him out on such a terrible evening.

'He is in such a lot pain though he won't admit it,' she told the doctor. 'I know my dad, he never ever complains but if you had seen him earlier when I first came in.'

Robert added his apologies to those of Sharon's and again tried to rise. The doctor wanted to examine him lying flat but Robert could not stand, let alone climb the stairs to his bedroom. He flatly rejected any suggestion of an ambulance to hospital for an x-ray. 'I aint fallen down and bruk mi leg, have I? Eventually she gave him a pain-killing injection and left promising to contact the consultant, though not offering any consolation of immediate surgery. When she left, Sharon picked up her telephone again.

By eleven o'clock that night, Robert was in a bed downstairs in the front room of his home. While Sharon prepared a meal, her brothers came, brought down a single bed from upstairs and ignoring his protests by feigning total deafness had carried him from the armchair to the bed.

The only concession made was to leave him alone for the night once they were satisfied he was reasonably comfortable.

Peace at last. He lay in the unfamiliar darkness, the pain reduced to a dull ache. Tomorrow Sharon would return and try to convince him that between herself and her brothers they could and would afford private surgery for him. Robert closed his eyes. His thoughts returned to Doris and the afternoon. He recalled holding her close as they waltzed around the dance floor. Drifting off to sleep, the music wafting through his head, he thought again of how he could contact her to make arrangements for the following week. As sleep finally overtook him, he remembered that some time ago he had given her his telephone number. He also remembered thinking then, 'Funny she never give me hers.'

12

Doris awoke feeling depressed. Not for many years had she felt less like getting out of bed than she did that morning. She turned towards the curtained window listening to the sound of the rain beating against it. Groaning inwardly she wondered if it was ever going to stop. Their agreement was to meet at the cafe on a Wednesday morning, have a cup of tea and then catch a bus to a destination chosen the previous week. Anne-Marie, Michel and Francois had served her tea and observed her eagerly scanning the road outside on two successive Wednesday mornings. They had shaken their heads sadly at each other when Doris, her head down, left the cafe. 'Perhaps it is this awful weather,' sighed Anne-Marie.

Since returning home following her second unsuccessful visit to the cafe on the Parade, it had rained almost without ceasing. The sky had been overcast most days and the rain was accompanied by high winds that caused the clouds to scud across the sky, branches to be torn from trees and litter to soar high before piling up as sodden masses in the gutter. Rain alternated between a steady drizzle and an almost torrential downpour. It filled the drains and gushed alongside the kerb until it flooded over to create puddles on badly maintained pavements.

Each day as she prepared to go out, Doris's thoughts had returned to the huddled figure of Robert limping away from the bus stop. She recalled rapping on the glass, then hastily removing her woollen glove to rap louder. But the bus had continued on while Robert disappeared into the darkness as a sense of foreboding descended upon her. It gradually deepened to a depression that she felt unable to shake off. She could see no way of solving her dilemma. Indeed, it had become a problem to which no solution seemed forthcoming.

'Oh that was a lovely, lovely afternoon,' she told herself when she eventually reached home. 'But poor dear Robert looked exhausted and in such pain. I know I have his number somewhere, I'll give him a ring tomorrow to see how he is. Perhaps if he is not well enough to come out, I could go to his house. Yes, that is what I'll do. He asked me if I wanted to.'

As soon as she had taken off her wet clothes, she emptied her bag. It was a long time since the contents had been so thoroughly sorted out. Each crumpled receipt, every scrap of paper was smoothed out flat and laid on the kitchen table. Loose coins were pulled from the folds of the lining. A broken pencil and an empty ballpoint pen emerged. Screwed up, disintegrating tissues plus a packet of 'Wet Wipes' were laid beside the purse and the pension book in its mock leather holder. A clear plastic wallet with her name, address and details of her next of kin caused a shadow of a smile to appear briefly on her lips when she remembered the family's insistence that she carry this information in the bag. 'Supposing something happens to you when you are out, mum.'

'Something like what?' had been her response.

'Oh you know.'

Neither her daughter, Joan, nor her brothers were forthcoming about the dark thoughts they wanted to protect their mother from. Nonetheless she did as they asked and kept it tucked in one of the internal pockets. A nail file, her bus pass and library tickets were added to the growing array. Some snapshots of the grandchildren. An elephant on an empty key ring. Which one of them gave it to her? Oh, yes, it was from a Christmas cracker. Little Simon was insistent that she take it. Door keys and a pair of small flat keys that would probably open all the locks on cheap suitcases the world over.

Surveying the contents of the now empty bag, Doris contemplated for a moment how trivial most of it was. Indeed at that moment none of it was important. She pushed all but the pieces of paper aside and began again to go through them. The ink on the majority of the paper scraps was indecipherable. None revealed a telephone number. Putting her hand deep inside the bag she pulled at the lining. The fabric gave way in her hand. 'Time I bought a new one I suppose. This one is an old friend though. Aah, what's this?' A ball of green and white paper fell from the corner. Eagerly she scrabbled at it. Smoothing and smoothing until the white inner side lay before her. She peered at it. Bent her head until it was almost touching the table. Yes this was the scrap of mint wrapper Robert gave her. However, the lead markings were faded with time and now there was nothing to see. 'Damn, damn, damn. What can I do now?' She supposed that she could ring directory enquiries.

Dialling the number, she gave the operator Robert's name and his district. 'I'm sorry you will have to give me more details than that.'

'I don't have any more,' she whispered into the receiver.

'Well you can imagine how many Robert Williams there are. Literally hundreds of them. What is name of the road?'

'I'm not sure.'

'I'm sorry,' said the operator.

Doris replaced the receiver in its cradle. 'What now?' she asked herself.

No immediate answer came to mind. Why hadn't she written the number in her address book as soon as she had returned home after babysitting for her family? Silly really.

Perhaps she was being unreasonably hard on herself. She had not wanted the family to find the number and to question her about it. They could, she knew, identify all the numbers in the book. Now her foolish pride was costing her dear. She hadn't ever given Robert her own number because she harboured a fear that he might call when one of the family was there to answer the telephone. That was another thing they always did. Answer her telephone in her house as if any calls would be for them.

But the weekly outings had become so much a part of her routine. Monday she always did her ironing before walking to the paper shop to buy her magazine. The first Monday of the month she would call in at the hairdresser on the way home and make an appointment for the following week to have her hair shampooed and trimmed. On Tuesdays and Thursdays there was lunch club with Amy. When they left the club on Tuesdays they usually called in to see an old friend who was housebound. Each Thursday they waited for the mobile library before parting to go to their own homes. And on Friday, Doris caught the bus into Brixton to buy fresh vegetables, wet fish and potter around in Morleys. Her children didn't like her going into Brixton to shop. They often reproached her saying that they feared for her safety. Doris's reply had been to point out that she was just one of hundreds of little old ladies who went shopping in town centres each week and that more of them died from natural causes than from standing in a queue behind a lady from the Caribbean buying up ten pounds of red mullet. Besides, where else could you get fresh wet fish from?

Once a month her eldest son John took her to the local supermarket in Crystal Palace where she stocked up on groceries. Doris, however, had grown to enjoy her independence. She did not intend giving up her weekly forays among the market stalls.

Going anywhere wasn't very pleasant when it rained, though Doris had to admit that she would have gone out in a howling blizzard to meet Robert any day of the week. She really looked forward to their jaunts, surprising herself at how bold she'd become. She and Amy often joked about the men who came to the club they attended. Sometimes they were like a couple of teenage girls giggling together over balding heads, a choice of aftershave or a garish sweater that a certain widow had knitted for an intended beau. Amy's wicked sense of humour was not above the odd sexual innuendo. She regarded herself as almost a widow, having divorced her husband after three years of marriage and gone to live with a man that she'd never married but to whom she had remained faithful unto death. There were no children, not that it bothered Amy who was as independent as she was forthright.

Not in her wildest flights of fantasy or rare moments of loneliness before Robert, had Doris ever thought of living with a man again. The chance meeting with Robert that gradually developed into a friendship, a companionship, made her realize that she could have a closeness with someone other than her family. She wished she could talk of her new relationship. Was that the right word? To young people relationships involved sex. She and Robert walked arm in arm, held hands. They had kissed.

Rolling over flat onto her back, her eyes fixed on the ceiling, her hand moved away from her body and explored the empty space beside her. She smoothed the cool flat sheet drawing it towards the pillow where it lingered. How long? Her hand moved down again. Closing her eyes she tried to imagine Robert lying beside her. With a gasp she sat up covering her face, as the realisation of the depths of her feelings dawned. Could she tell her children and Amy? If Robert were not a Jamaican, would she hold the same doubts about telling them?

Did his family know about her? He often talked about his children. Of his struggle to bring them up on his own. Of his boyhood in Jamaica and how he travelled to England via Spain on a boat that docked at Southampton in falling snow. He and his travelling companions almost missed the train to Waterloo because they stopped to feel and marvel at the soft white stuff that fell soundlessly from the heavens. She sensed that her children would not like anyone to come between her and their inheritance. They often made decisions for her, informing her of the forthcoming holiday booked or which day one of them would be coming to collect her for a meal.

When their father died, it had been a while before she had been able to assert any measure of independence at all. There was a stage when she felt like shouting at them to go away and leave her in peace. She would have loved to have ignored the ringing door bell and the insistent burring of the telephone. Then a full scale S.A.S. assault on the house might have occurred as the family, convinced that she was dead in bed, or the victim of an attack in her home, despite all the security precautions taken to protect her, strove to 'look after' her.

Sighing, Doris pushed back the quilt, sat up and lowered her legs to the floor. How many weeks was it now? she wondered. How could she contact Robert and would she ever see him again?

Some two or three weeks in succession, she had returned to the cafe, sitting at the same table peering anxiously through the window, making a cup of tea last an hour, wishing, hoping, praying, please God let him come. But he didn't. Was it because there hadn't been the usual 'See you next week' when they parted? Was there any use in her going again today?

Drawing back the curtains, she looked down through the streaked glass and surveyed the grey landscape of her garden. The rain fell straight down like rods of water onto the sodden earth. Water dripped incessantly from the edge of the gutter pinging onto a planter before joining the pools lying in the hollows of the paving stones of the patio. Skeletal trees waved their bony fingers against an endless leaden sky bereft of bird or sunshine. At the bottom of the garden, a solitary cat sat stared balefully from beneath the shed doorway. 'I know how you feel,' thought Doris turning away from the gloomy picture and reaching for her robe.

In the bathroom, she stood before the mirror wondering what to do. What had she done on Wednesdays before Robert came into her life? Sitting down on the closed toilet seat her mind wandered back to that first meeting.

Eventually Doris stirred and began the daily ritual of preparing for the day. What was she preparing for? Today was Wednesday. Once a long time ago she had caught the bus up to the Palace on Wednesdays just to have an excuse for going out. She went for a cup of tea in the French cafe on Westow Street, then found some small item of grocery to buy in the supermarket before journeying home. That was how she had met Robert.

I don't even need to get dressed today, she thought, drifting from bathroom to bedroom and then downstairs. Pausing to pick up the solitary letter lying on the carpet, Doris entered her kitchen. A few moments later sitting at the table, coffee mug steaming in front of her, she began going through the same strategies she had contemplated since watching him disappear, limping into the darkness that evening after the dance.

'Pull yourself together,' she told herself for the umpteenth time. 'You are behaving like a lovesick girl.'

A lump swelled in her throat. Her eyes began to prick with the effort of holding back tears that she knew were impossible to stem. Her eyes swam. They travelled to the window and beyond. Her misery increased as the rain intensified and began to lash against the glass. Laying her head upon the table she abandoned herself to tears.

13

A wet November was followed by a bitterly cold December. Although there were only a few days of frost, the trees in Robert's garden became images of bridesmaids decked in white lace at a wedding. And the untended dead bedding plants stood blackened and rigid on icing sugar dusted earth. It was the icy cold winds that appeared to be blowing straight from Siberia that caused people standing at bus stops to huddle, bundled in hoods and scarves, against walls and fences and in shop doorways still shivering. There seemed to be no escaping the bone-chilling wind. Robert, despite the pain of his crumbling hip, knew also the despair of not being able to contact Doris. She had his telephone number but he didn't have hers. He'd kept meaning to ask her.

Now he regretted this oversight because not only did he feel that he was letting her down, he also realized how much he wanted to see her. He could not understand why she had not called him. Throughout the time that they had been travelling around London together he had come to enjoy her company. If anyone had asked him his feelings for Doris, he would not have admitted to any notion of being romantically involved. Whenever his children teased him about his 'likkle girlfriend,' he brushed off the suggestion. He gave nothing away. He did not even allow himself a second thought.

Reaching out for the mango that lay in a small dish on the table beside him, he lifted it to his nose. He held it in the palm of his hand. He sniffed the dry, wrinkled skin. A thin layer of grey mould covered the large black indentation that spread downwards from the stem. When Sharon brought home the mango along with his usual weekly shopping, its green skin tinged with red, had been firm and smooth.

'Give this a couple of days, daddy,' she told him, laying it carefully on the paper napkin-lined dish, with a small sharp knife beside it. 'I know how you love a ripe mango.'

The mango lay uneaten for three weeks. Each day Robert held it, running his hands over the softening skin. He watched it change from green to red, from red to orange, from orange to yellow mottled with black. The smooth shiny skin gradually transformed until it was shrivelled and wrinkled. When he slowly and painfully made his way into the room every morning, his spirits were lifted by the sweet aroma that greeted him.

'Today,' he told himself optimistically.

The soft fruit almost touched his nostrils as he tried in vain to recapture the elusive scent, to relive that moment in Richmond Park, the kiss, the taste, the feel of her arms.

His eyes burned with unshed tears and a lump formed in his throat. Despair and frustration now replaced the earlier optimism. His grasp on the mango tightened and the parched skin gave way as his fingers dug deeper and deeper. Yellow fibres oozed through his dark brown fingers, pushed beneath his nails, hung from his palm and mingled with the shredded skin. He used the napkin to wipe his hand clean before limping into the kitchen.

Long after he had returned to his chair, the pungent aroma of ripe mango filled the room.

Like the episode in the park, the tea dance was an unforgettable experience for Robert clouded only by the pain that followed. He sat in his chair close to the gas fire, recalling the way in which she had rested her head on his shoulder, the firm grasp of her hand as they walked onto the dance floor and the closeness of her body next to his when they waltzed beneath the sparkling lights. It was a long time since he had been physically close to anyone. When Nadia, the mother of his children abandoned them by walking out of their lives, he had vowed never to become involved with another woman. He had kept that promise through the years of being both mother and father. He had become accustomed to celibacy and to some extent loneliness. His friends gradually stopped telephoning or calling unannounced for him to go for a drink or a game of Bingo because he would not leave the children alone in the house.

Only when they were teenagers and beginning to take some responsibility for themselves did he once again start to have the occasional drink and game of dominoes at the local pub. When he joined the local Black Pensioners club on his retirement, the long lost friends greeted him as if he were the ancient mariner returned from years at sea. It was good to be part of the circle again but he maintained the reserve that had grown over the years and also the resolve not to get romantically involved. Until the meeting at Paxton Green roundabout.

Robert had argued at length with his children about having his hip replacement done privately. Eventually they capitulated and accepted his view that he had contributed to the National Health service from the day after he arrived in the country.

The day after arriving in London his cousin had taken him to the Labour Exchange, given him some advice and left him. Robert told the thin bespectacled man who coughed as if he was about to expire that he was a trained carpenter. He showed the sniffing spectre his papers proving that he had completed a formal apprenticeship. They were ignored. Instead, he directed Robert to a local factory where for three months he swept the iron filings from the floor and ran bogus errands after which he returned bewildered and angry to the laughing workers attending the machinery.

Every evening he returned to the room shared with his cousin and vowed to look for another job. And as his anger grew, so did his determination. Eventually he had taken a day off and returned to the Labour Exchange. This time he did not go directly to the counter until after reading the rows of cards fastened to the notice boards lining the room. He carefully wrote down details of positions that he felt applied to his skills and then approached the counter determined not to leave until he was satisfied.

To his surprise, the person he spoke to, a young woman with her hair piled high in a beehive and a sweater so tight her breasts appeared to be attempting to burst through the thin fabric, filled out the necessary details and handed him the addresses of two of the vacancies. Already dressed in a suit, with white shirt, collar and tie, Robert boarded a bus to the local hospital. After several attempts at finding his way to the personnel officers' room, he finally asked a tall skinny Jamaican woman wearing a green striped overall where to go. He remembered her distinctly with that mop and bucket in her hand.

Twenty minutes after entering the dingy office that smelt as if the single window had never been opened since the hospital was built, Robert emerged employed as a maintenance carpenter. Three weeks later he moved into his own room on the third floor of a house round the corner from where his cousin lodged. The room contained a bed, dressing table and a huge wardrobe. He bought a green paraffin heater, a gallon of paraffin, two saucepans, a cup and saucer, a knife, fork and spoon and two enamel plates. On the window sill in his room he kept a tray covered with a tea towel on which were a tin of condensed milk, a packet of tea and a tea strainer. The water for his tea was heated in the smallest of the two pans perched on top of the little heater. So was the milk he used to make a bowl of thick oat porridge each morning. The only time he used the communal cooker that was down stairs on the next landing was on a Sunday when he prepared sufficient stew peas and rice and chicken to last him until Tuesday.

The remaining days he ate in the cafe across the road from the hospital with the two men who worked in the boiler room. One was a Barbadian who had joined the Royal Air Force during the war and then chosen to stay in London. The other was a stooping old English man whose permanently unlit cigarette hung as if welded to his bottom lip. A local man, for some reason he had taken a liking to the 'Blackies' who turned up on time everyday whatever the weather.

The weeks soon passed. He knew his way around the hospital, from the dingy attics below the roofs, to the maze of store rooms in the basements where broken-down beds and other equipment lay abandoned to the dust and whatever stray cat found its way in.

One grey afternoon he left the tiny cupboard that was supposed to be the maintenance office and walked through a steady drizzle across the courtyard into the hospital building, glad to leave the gloomy hole that reeked of stale tobacco and male sweat mingled with oil and new wood. He carried his brown canvas bag of tools with him. Tools that had travelled across the Atlantic in a wooden box made by him when he began to learn the trade with his uncle back home.

The box now remained with a battered suitcase under his bed. He was going to replace a door handle on one of the wards. There were several people waiting near the lift peering at the wrought iron gates as if to will the ancient lift down even faster. As he climbed the three flights of stairs, Robert heard it groaning and rattling when it passed shuddering to the ground floor. Pushing open the wooden double doors, he saw the skinny Jamaican woman again. She was mopping the corridor, head down, arms moving purposefully in a wide swinging movement that took the long cotton strands of the mop from one wall to the other. Feet planted firmly apart she executed a peculiar backward shuffle as her body was propelled towards the inner door of the ward. Looking neither right nor left, she lifted the mop, plunged it into the bucket and swilled it around while she pulled it with her down the corridor. The mop was then squeezed firmly in the colander-like device on top of the bucket and with a swish, the motion began again accompanied by a litany understood only by those heralding from the same part of the world as she. The ward sister, staff nurse and dogsbodies translated her sounds into grumbles and moans about having to clear up after 'Dem hinglish people,' when she 'lef home to train in nursing.'

The green-striped dress was firmly tied about a waist so thin Robert could have spanned it with his two hands. On the lowered head was perched a cap similar to those worn by the nurses though it did not display a coloured band as theirs did.

'Afternoon, Mistress.'

'I aint no Mistress,' she responded slapping the mop hard onto the floor.

'Beg pardon, my deah.'

'I aint your deah neither.'

Taking a shuffle back, bucket in tow, she sniffed loudly. He ignored her and continued into the ward.

For the next hour he worked on the door of the sister's office moving around on his knees every time she or a doctor entered or left. He kept his eyes firmly on his work though his ears were tuned to all that was said whether it was about a patient or a member of the ward staff. When the job was completed, he asked for a dustpan and brush to sweep up the wood shavings and dust that had accumulated on the floor.

'Miss Battley will get it for you,' he was told. A few moments later, the angry young woman in the green-striped dress appeared.

Without looking at him, she thrust the brush and pan into his hands mumbling about, 'People too lazy to get tings for deyself.' Robert should have realized then what Nadia was like, but he was lonely for a woman's company and besides, she struck him as being full of life, unlike the young stolid looking girls who were training to be nurses here in the hospital.

He ignored the anger in her voice and caught hold of her slim wrist with his free hand while grasping the handle of the pan with the other. Now she looked at him and as she did so, recognition dawned.

'Yu get de job, den?'

This was the woman who was to later move in with him and eventually leave him with four children to rear on his own. She was the reason he upped his five pound a week 'pardner' contribution to ten pound, in order to raise a deposit for a house of their own. The house in which he still lived.

Robert continued at the hospital until he retired. He was presented with a testimonial and a gold watch which he never wore but looked at everyday when he woke to a new and unaccustomed idleness. Even now, when getting up and out from bed was such a painful and laborious business, he would turn his head to the watch, still on the stand it had been wrapped around. He would check the time. He also looked at it again when he finally stood panting on his stick and began to shuffle towards the downstairs toilet, noting mentally just how long it had taken him to get upright.

Sitting by the fire listening to the radio or dozing, Robert awakened with thoughts of Doris. What must she be thinking of him now? Perhaps this was what she wanted. Was this a way to lose contact with him or to get rid of him and end their weekly journeys? No, this couldn't be so because she was the one who always suggested where they should go the following week and she had suggested the tea dance and the swimming. Still, despite the many hours he spent thinking about her and the pleasant times they had shared together, he could not see how to solve his problem of getting in touch with her.

He wondered if Doris was feeling the same way and if she would find a means to contact him. She knew he lived just around the corner from the bus stop and she must have seen the direction he took each time they parted. But unless she tramped up and down the road knocking on doors, and she was not the sort of woman to do that, she could hardly find him. Would he do as much for her? Yes, he told himself, he most definitely would. Not that there was any chance of being able to do it now. He cursed his hip and the enforced invalidity. What was there to do?

He heard the rattle of the letterbox and the soft plop of the post as it dropped onto the mat. Almost simultaneously the telephone placed strategically at his elbow on the tallest of his nesting tables rang loudly, startling him out of his reverie. He almost dropped it in his haste. To his surprise, it was the admissions' clerk from the hospital telling him that there would be a bed for him the day after Boxing day and could he come in for the pre-operation tests. He agreed without hesitation, then, trembling, he groped for a pen to take down the details the woman was giving him. Laying down the receiver, he gazed out of the window into the gathering twilight. The wind pushing heavy clouds across the darkening sky bent the bare trees. Robert was overcome with confusion. He desperately wanted the hip replacement operation. Anything, even amputation would be preferable to the constant pain he was in.

Yet what he would have liked to happen even more than that, was to be able to contact Doris and tell her how much he missed her.

The telephone which sat upon two directories caught his eye. 'Of course, what a fool ting me is. Why me didn tink of it before.' He moved the telephone to one side and began turning the yellow pages of the first directory. After a few moments he realised his mistake and for the first time in many weeks chuckled to himself. 'Me wont find her name in dis one, will I? Now, Mistress Thomas let me see.' The heavy dark blue tome almost slipped from his grasp as with eager hands he began again to turn the pages.

An hour passed. Robert sat, head bent, muttering to himself in the yellow glow of the table lamp. With his inability to find a number in the area in which he knew Doris lived, his frustration became palpable. Sighing audibly, he closed the book. His hands lingered on the cover.

'Is jus like goin round dem blasted roundabouts an not gettin anywhere.'

Glancing down at his hands, his eyes caught the wording beneath them: Residential Lewisham.

'Ah, no wonder you can't find no Mistress Thomas address in dere. She don't live in de borough of Lewisham. She live in Lambeth. Tomorrow, I will call the phone people dem an aks dem to send me a directory for her borough. Me been going roun an roun di wrong way all de time.'

Another Wednesday drew to a close. Robert, trembling with excitement reached for his calender. Taking his pen, he marked off the day before counting backwards the number of days that had passed since he last saw Doris.

15

When in early December Doris found herself embroiled in family preparations for Christmas, she recalled that there had previously been some discussion about it during August. Her involvement and preoccupatiom with Robert meant she had given the conversation scant attention. Now she remembered her eldest daughter insisting that everyone make up their minds soon because she needed to book a place while there was still vacancies, particularly as they were such a large family group. What Doris could not remember was saying that she wanted to be included. However, reservations had been made and now she was very aware that she was included. She pondered what the reaction might be if she declared at this late stage that she did not want to join them and intended spending Christmas at home. The thought was actually quite a pleasant one marred only by not being in contact with Robert.

On her worst days (The Wednesdays now spent at home) Doris dared to imagine herself and Robert sitting quietly in her kitchen toasting each other a 'Happy Christmas'. Even beginning a New Year together. She would rouse from these daily dreams and remind herself just how impossible the thought was. Her family would never approve.

Joan and her husband had succeeded in persuading the rest of the family that hiring a cottage in Wales was a novel way to spend the festive season. 'I know you'll love it, mum, all of us being together; one big, happy family,' she had announced. She reinforced her argument by reminding them that they all visited each other over the holiday week, using up petrol and physical energy. So why shouldn't they drive a few hundred miles and enjoy Christmas without distractions. 'At least we get all the driving over in one foul swoop.' Foul was a most apt word, indeed, thought Doris. Who in their right mind would want to drive across England to a cottage on a remote seashore in the middle of winter?

As usual the final decision was made and Doris was informed when a suitably sized residence was booked, the deposit paid and the driving arrangements finalized. It occurred to her that as much work was going into Christmas in Wales as it was into spending it at home.

One whole Sunday afternoon and evening was spent in her sitting room, 'It's time we visited you anyway, mum', planning meals, drawing up shopping lists, deciding who would share a room with whom and at what time and in whose car people would travel. Then there was the question of Christmas stockings and presents, how much money they should spend on each other and was it worth buying each other Christmas cards?

Doris retreated to the kitchen with Billy, her grandson to prepare tea. Billy decided to make a sponge cake while Doris buttered bread for sandwiches and made custard for a trifle.

'Do you really think it will be easier for us all if we go away for Christmas, Nan?' He deftly wiped the rubber spatula around the mixing bowl and plonked the last of the mixture in the tins before wiping his finger across it and licking it.

'What does your Cookery teacher say when you do that?' asked Doris laughing.

'She knows we do it but says that she better not catch us at it, especially in exams. And, Nan, it's not called Cookery anymore. It's Food Technology.'

Doris sniffed. 'When I was at school it was known as Housecraft and when your mother did it they called it Domestic Science. What's the difference?'

'We only do cooking now, Nan, not washing and ironing and housework.'

'No wonder the young people of today don't know how to look after themselves.'

'Nan', Billy interrupted, 'What do you think about this holiday idea? You weren't saying much in there.'

'No-one asked me what my opinion was. But if I don't go with all of you I will be here on my own, won't I?'

'What about your friends, Nan?' Billy was washing up the equipment he had used.

'Oh most of them have families and Amy is going to visit a friend in America. There is one person though.' She turned away from the table to reach for a large plate on which to pile the filled sandwiches. Resuming her place, she continued buttering slices of bread.

'Who's that, then?' He opened and shut first the refrigerator and then various cupboard doors as he began to gather together the ingredients for the frosting.

'Oh you wouldn't know him. Besides, I seem to have lost touch with him. Anyway, he has family. Though it would be nice to see him again.'

'Who, Nan?'

Doris, thinking that she was saying too much, tried to change the subject by asking Billy about school.

Billy persisted. 'You said 'he', Nan, does that mean you have a boyfriend?'

'Can't I meet people without you implying that I am doing wrong?'

'I didn't say there was anything wrong. I was just curious.'

There was a special affinity between Doris and her eldest grandson, very different to how she had been with her own children, and not the same as her feelings towards the other younger three. She realised that she needed to confide in somebody, to talk about how miserable she felt most days and how she missed her meetings with Robert.

'Look, Billy this is just between you and me. It is not a life or death secret and it won't be the end of the world if you tell your mother though for some reason I would rather none of them knew. They seem to think that I am not capable of making decisions for myself.'

'Okay, Nan, I wont tell anyone.' Winking at her, he tiptoed to the door and pretended to check there was no-one listening.

'Be serious, Bill.' He returned to the table assuring her that he was.

'I do have a special friend, Billy. Well I did have. But somehow we seem to have lost touch.' A lump formed in her throat and her eyes filled. She turned away and opened a drawer, fumbling inside, not wanting him to see.

Billy waited. Silence filled the kitchen that seemed at that moment a thousand miles away from the rest of the family in the next room. He saw the desolation that swept over her face and he sensed his grandmother's sadness. He was relieved when the timer on the cooker shrilled and disturbed the quiet at the same time as he could clearly smell the cake.

While his back was turned, Doris wiped her eyes. Clearing her throat, she told him that she had got to know someone and that the last time she saw him he wasn't well. She didn't know where he lived so she couldn't get in touch with him.

'Silly really, an old woman like me getting upset over someone she met in the street.' She added to a second neat pile of sandwiches mounting on the bread board.

'You're not old, Nan. If he was a good friend, why didn't you give him your telephone number?'

'I have asked myself that a thousand times.'

'Do you like him a lot?'

Billy lifted the second cake tin from the oven and laid it on the cooling rack. He listened while his grandmother spoke of her fondness for her friend. Doris carefully drew the bread knife across the bread and sunk it deep into the soft white mass.

'I suppose I do. We enjoyed each other's company and I have never met anyone like him before.'

She was aware that she meant it in more ways than the one implied.

'Do you want to find him again? Is there anything I can do to help, Nan?'

He realised that this person was obviously more than just a friend.

'Just listening to me has helped, Bill.' She turned away from him.

Over tea everyone seemed to be talking at once. They appeared to have settled most of the vital issues. Doris sat in her usual place at the head of the table. A space that her husband had occupied for many years and that she, unable to bring herself to sit on the chair or face the emptiness, had left vacant for a long time after his death. She took to eating in the kitchen or from a tray on her lap, something he had frowned upon. Then as the grandchildren outgrew the high chair and needed to sit at the table with the rest of the family when they visited her, Doris found a place laid for her in dad's old place. Now whichever child laid the table they always placed her at the head. From that position she poured tea, passed plates, served food and surveyed her noisy, bossy children. How had it come about that they, not her, were in command?

After the funeral, on her return to the empty house, she had tried to insist that she was fine and would be able to manage on her own. Somehow they never took it on board. And gradually she had grown to accept her children directing her life and making decisions for her though. At the same time, she tried to maintain some degree of independence over her daily routines and also where she shopped. That was until she encountered Robert. If Doris was positive about anything, it was that meeting him was her turning point. She began to realize that there were choices to be made and that she could choose to organize her own life. So for a while now, Doris had begun to quietly assert her independence a little more.

As she sat engulfed by words (though momentarily alone and oblivious), she became aware that the family were discussing sleeping arrangements. Rousing from her thoughts she spoke, startling both children and grandchildren.

'I hope that I will have a room to myself in this cottage. If we are going to be spending nearly a week cooped up together miles from anywhere in what might be appalling weather, I think that at my age, I should be allowed a space to retreat.'

'Wow', she thought, 'that got 'em.'

'Good for you, Nan.' Though everyone else was stunned, Billy's thumbs up sign accompanied by a wink showed that he approved.

'Well, mum,' Joan began.

'No buts, Joan. Whenever we go away on holiday I always share with one of the children. No-one consults me. You all just assume that I won't mind.' Taking a deep breath, Doris continued headlong. She disallowed any interruptions.

'This is different. There is going to be quite a crowd which means it will be noisy and I feel that I should have a place to rest and have a bit of peace and quiet if I want it.'

Attempting reparation she added, 'Hope that doesn't cause any offence. But I'm sure you can you see what I mean.'

'I think Gran is quite right.'

'This has nothing to do with you, Billy,' his father said sharply.

Billy closed his mouth but winked again at his grandmother. Doris, surprised by her own boldness wished that she could have added that she wasn't going anyway, that she was planning to spend the festive season with a dear friend. Yes, that's just what he was, a dear, dear friend. If only she could find a way to contact him.

15

Robert tried to curb his impatience while he awaited the arrival of the telephone directory he had ordered. Daily as he sat trying to read either a newspaper or a book, he was distracted by his thoughts. He imagined finding the number, calling Doris, telling her what had happened since their last meeting, and arranging for her to come and visit him at home. Opening his door to her. If only the telephone book would come.

He tried to conjure up other routes to find and contact her. But except for ringing the cafe, they all involved being mobile. The staff there must know who he wanted them to pass a message to. Surely they would do that for him. After all, he and Doris were regulars. Yes, another avenue leading from the roundabout appeared to be opening up. But first he would try contacting her directly, though. If he found the number in the book and her address, he could also write to her.

Closing his eyes he began to compose a letter: My dear Mistress Thomas... No that was too formal. Hello Doris? Dear Doris or Dearest Doris. He wondered if he should apologise for not contacting her, or say how much he missed her and wanted to see her again. He considered that she might possibly be offended because he had not been in contact for such a long time. Perhaps a card was better. Sharon could buy one for him. An open card with a picture of roses. Doris liked roses. Then he need only put his address and telephone number inside and sign his name. No, there had to be a message. Brief, simple:

> Dear Doris,
> How are you? Please get in touch with me.
> Love, Robert.

Love. How would she accept that word? He thought of their holding hands, their kissing. Closing a card with love was surely acceptable. After that, it was up to her to contact him. Two simple roads leading from the roundabout to her. Not long now, he told himself. Not long before I see her again.

He dragged an old ruler painstakingly down the columns of names searching through Thomas, Thompson, Thomason, Tompkins and finally Tompkinson. He double checked initials looking for an F or a D. Using a street map, he checked the road names against those that looked promising in the directory. But all to no avail.

Anger and frustration welled up inside him. He hit the open pages of the directory before summoning up enough strength to hurl it to the floor.

'All me seem to meet is dead ends,' he groaned.

As he sat worrying himself, it didn't even cross Robert's mind that Doris's number might be ex-directory.

16

While Doris prepared for a Christmas within the bosom of her family, Robert and his children made preparations for his stay in hospital. He would rather they forgot about it until Christmas was over. Instead every sentence referred to before or after 'your operation'. Sharon, who was spending more time with him than in her own home presented him with three nightshirts, declaring them to be an early Christmas present. As she held each one up in turn for him to approve, she assured him that they would be more comfortable than pyjamas. Robert, eyeing the red tartan of one, the forest green paisley pattern of the second and the yellow with blue stripes of the third was not so sure.

'Me caan wear those without pants and if I wear mi pants I might as well wear proper pyjamas.'

'Oh, daddy, you don't need to worry about anyone seeing you. The nurses are quite used to looking at a man's equipment.'

She pranced around the room holding one of the garments against her.

'You know what, daddy, when you are better I think I will have these for myself. They look great. What do you think?'

'Don't be disrespectful to your father, Sharon. What I got down dere is private an I aint goin into no hospital to show it off to girls young enough to be me grans.' He refused to be distracted, so Sharon folded them back into the bag promising herself to see that they were packed into the case he was taking with him. His children were concerned about their father. Steven telephoned Devon who lived in America, not only to inform him of the forthcoming operation but also to discuss the depressive mood swings that Robert seemed to have developed lately.

He had never been a noisy or demonstrative man, none of them could ever recall him really showing emotion. When they misbehaved as children he would usually send them to their room to think about the misdemeanour, while promising to deal with it later. Dealing with it meant extracting a promise never to do it again, because if they even thought about it he would use the belt on them. The threat was enough. He had never laid a finger on any of them.

The only time his children recalled seeing Robert upset was the day their mother abandoned them at the child minder's house. Arriving late to collect them full of apologies, flustered because he had no excuse to offer, he bundled them home. He fed and bathed them and called them to sit on his bed.

He did not know where she was but all her clothes were gone. He could not say if she would be coming back and he did not know what would happen to them. Then he stood in the doorway of each room and watched as they climbed into bed, said goodnight and turned out the lights.

The following morning, after a night spent pacing the floor, he awakened his four children aged between two and seven years, washed dressed and breakfasted them and took them to the minder. With a face like granite he told the minder the reason for his lateness the day before. He kissed the children and continued on his way to work. He never mentioned their mother again.

He repelled all advice from friends, told the social workers he could manage, resisted all enquiries by them and refused any offers of help. He told the head teacher of the boys' primary school that his business was to educate his children not to mind his family's affairs. The children were warned not to discuss home at school and the teachers instructed where he could be found should there be an emergency. If Devon, Aston, Steven and Sharon were bewildered at the sudden disappearance of their mother, they were not able to talk with Robert, who pulled down a blind on that aspect of his life and became both mother and father to his little family.

Each child, even Sharon the baby was given a household chore. As they grew older, the amount of housework or allotted tasks increased. Thus from initially muddling along, Robert and his children became self-sufficient. Robert had always been able to prepare meals because his mother, unlike her neighbours in their small community in Jamaica let him help as a child in her kitchen. The meals he cooked for his children were basic: ox-tail soup with butter beans, yam, eddoes and rock hard sticky dumplings; liver and onions accompanied by mounds of steaming white rice; corned beef, cabbage, yam and green bananas; fresh mackerel, seasoned and fried, eaten with boiled plantain, potatoes and occasionally spinach. On Sundays he fried chicken and prepared red beans and rice sufficient to last through to Monday. Every dish except for the stew was accompanied by a salad of lettuce and tomatoes. He insisted all four ate breakfast before leaving the house and each evening prepared a cup of hot sweet Milo for supper when they went to bed.

Washing for his young family entailed a trip to the local launderette, pushing the entire week's laundry balanced on Sharon's pushchair. While the washing revolved and spun, Robert took the children into the library next door to change and select their books. When the washing was dry, folded and loaded onto the pushchair all five trekked home. Devon, the eldest, made everyone a sandwich while their father hung up the clothes to air. Then they left the house again to walk to Lewisham to do the weekly shopping. They returned laden, Sharon pushed by her father and hidden beneath bags and packages. Her brothers struggled with carrier bags trying not to drag them on the ground.

On Sundays Robert insisted that they went to Sunday school. He wasn't sure if this was to inculcate Christian beliefs or to give himself an hour's peace and quiet. Devon as the eldest had the responsibility of shepherding the little family to the nearest chapel. He became an expert in crowd control early in his young life especially after the pushchair finally gave up the ghost under the weight of the washing and shopping and Sharon had to walk everywhere.

Through trial and error, Robert eventually mastered the art of braiding Sharon's hair. There were mornings when he used the stiff bristled brush with such vigour that his young daughter squealed and wriggled like a piglet. Those days she usually left the house with her hair scraped up on the top of her head into one bunch held fast by a tightly wound elastic band. He vowed that come the next Saturday, when the boys visited the barber, hers would be cut too. Then his memories of home would surface and he knew that it was tantamount to a deadly sin to cut a girl's hair. Wasn't it Solomon who said that a woman's hair was her crowning glory? His resolve broken, he would try again and again to part, oil and braid the mass of unruly hair. Pride would not let him ask anyone the best way to deal with it, or, indeed to do it for him. So for months Sharon suffered, dreading the daily ritual as much as he did.

On one of the rare occasions when he talked to his children about his own boyhood, he recalled his grandmother sitting on the wooden steps outside his home in Jamaica, her own head tightly wrapped in white cotton, unlit pipe in mouth, his sister's head held firmly between her knees as she first undid the braids. Then, without the aid of a brush she began to pull the comb through her hair. When Grandma was satisfied that every knot and tangle was removed, she commenced oiling. Judging from his sister's grimaces as her head went from side to side and up and down, this was almost as bad as the disentangling. Yet she dared not make a sound of protest. For those dextrous work-worn hands were just as capable of administering a sharp slap on the side of her head as they were of tenderly encouraging a newly born infant to take its first breath.

It was only when grandma began the parting and plaiting that his sister relaxed. Then he and the other children made themselves comfortable on and around the steps as grandma began to speak. In turn, each girl changed places and seated herself between the floral-patterned bony knees. Work-worn ebony fingers continued to brush and weave intricate patterns, (no head the same). Soon the stories flowed from grandma's lips like water from the standpipe, though arguably sweeter than the honey from granpa's beehives. Night fell and the peeniwallies dipped and flashed momentarily in the darkening sky. Grandma's voice lulled the youngest to sleep and the older children into a lazy stupor. The distant barking of dogs in the village and the occasional raucous laughter from the men playing dominoes only added to the atmosphere.

As darkness closed in, the magic was broken when his mother called for them to get to bed because they had to rise early for school the following day. Each girl's head was tightly tied in a torn off strip of fabric, safeguarding grandma's handiwork until the next time her skills were needed. He recalled being terrified of the duppies that grandma had told him about in the stories.

It was this memory of home that had caused Robert to begin doing Sharon's hair in the evenings after her bath. His own fingers could never compete with those of his grandmother's weaving that recalled a bygone time and a history of clan or kin. Neither did he tell stories to his children. Instead, as he struggled to section Sharon's hair into manageable amounts, he heard each of his children read from their school reading book. With the little girl's hair done, and before putting her to bed he tied it with an old headscarf that their mother had left behind. Unbeknown to him, Sharon had retained the scarf, now a battered remnant, lying folded beneath her underwear in a drawer in her own home. The only link with a person whose face she could not even remember.

For almost sixteen years Robert took responsibility for Sharon's hair. At the age of twelve, she began to care for it herself, washing and braiding it, adding beads when beads became fashionable. Weaving coloured thread among the black when she tired of the beads. He steadfastly resisted her pleas to let her relax it, in the same way he refused to let the boys grow Afros.

Then, when she returned home at the end of her first term in university, head almost shorn, he recalled those years, reminding her of how he had cared for her hair and this was how she repaid him. Her response was that she was old enough now to make decisions about her hair and could do what she liked with it. There was a period of changes from shorn to dyed hair when he berated her and warned her of the consequences of abusing her crowning glory. Finally, she began to twist the growing hair into locks, which although Robert would never admit to being in favour of, he was growing accustomed to.

Steven explained to his older brother about the times when his father relapsed into long periods of silence as if he were brooding over something.

'We've asked him many times to tell us if there is anything wrong, what we can do for him or if there is anyone he wants us to contact. Man, it's like there is something on his mind, you know.'

'Well, Steve, our Pa has never been one to really show or tell us what he is feeling. Remember when we were teenagers we used to call him Old Granite face?' Devon chuckled down the line.

'It's okay for you,' Steven grumbled. 'He won't let us pay for private treatment. He insists that he has paid his due. We know he is in pain but the way he is seems like he is depressed about something.'

'You don't think he's getting senile, do you?' There was a note of alarm in Devon's voice.

'No, it's like I said,' replied Steven. 'We think he has something on his mind but he can't find a way to sort it out.'

'You know how our father is, Steve. If he doesn't want us to know, he ain't going to tell us till he good and ready. And if he doesn't consider it any of our business then he won't and that's for definite.'

Steven sighed, preparing to say his good-byes.

'Hey, Steve, what happened to that girlfriend you all told me he had?'

'Devon, man, daddy never admitted to having a girlfriend and that's one thing he will positively not discuss with us. Not even with Sharon. And you know how she's the apple of his eye. She can tease him about most things but not that. Anyway, I think that if there was one, she's been off the scene for a while.'

'You sure about that, man? Maybe he missing some sugar that's why he seems depressed to all of you.'

'Since when were you the long distance psychiatrist? You need to be here. Then you will know what I'm getting at. And if daddy heard you talking about him like,' his voiced trailed off.

'Oh come on now, man, is joke I joking. You know that I'll be over the day he goes into hospital. Give him a kiss for me. I'll call you next week.'

Steven replaced the receiver. A frown creased his brow. Perhaps there was some truth in what his brother was saying. Anyway there was no way any of them could discuss it with their father. Neither was it possible for them to contact this friend, if she existed, because his father was certainly not forthcoming with any details.

17

Enforced idleness took its toll of Robert's health. Before long he developed a chest infection that needed treatment with antibiotics. The pain relief medication worked to a certain extent though at night he found it difficult to sleep. When he lay down to ease the pressure on his hip, his breathing became laboured. If he sat propped on pillows, his back stiffened and his hip began to throb. Consequently he was short with his family, cross with himself and curt to the doctor and the district nurse who came in to administer the twice daily injections during his first week of illness.

'One consolation,' Sharon reported to her brothers, 'is that all the medication is making him sleepy. So he doesn't keep moaning at me.'

The family's two concerns were: firstly, whether his mood might lift before Christmas and secondly, and most importantly, if he would be fit and well enough to undergo the major surgery scheduled for mid-January. There were, however, days when his depression lifted and he was able to discuss meals and shopping with his children. Those were the occasions when he continually reassured them that he was going to cook the Christmas dinner as usual. As the time drew near and he remained virtually immobile, he gave in to the niggling doubts and conceded, finally, that for the first time ever, someone else would be taking over his kitchen.

Eventually Sharon offered to come and stay on Christmas eve while the rest of the family would come, as was the tradition, on Christmas day.

'Daddy will help me. He can be the director from the chair.'

Boxing day they intended to maintain the familiar routine of Sharon driving her father to each of the brothers, in turn.

The days were long for Robert as he struggled to maintain his independence and stay out of hospital until the given date. His doctor threatened him with hospitalization if his chest didn't clear up. He knew the operation would not take place if he was still unwell. The difficulty was combating the pain sufficiently to keep fairly mobile and the 'damn tiredness doesn't help.'

Two days before Christmas he was startled from a doze by the ringing of the doorbell. Both the doctor and the nurse knew to walk round to the side of the house and enter through the kitchen door. So struggling to shake of the drowsiness, Robert fumbled for his stick while trying to rise from the chair. His lack of mobility frustrated him so that by the time he reached the hallway he was muttering loudly. The person on the other side of the door peered through the letterbox while calling his name.

'You dere Mr Williams? Hello, hellooo! Yu dere, brudder Robert? Is me. Come nah, man, open de door. Mi gettin cold out here.'

Recognizing the voice, he called, 'I comin, I comin. Hold on, now.'

Having ascertained that Robert was in, Sister Priscilla relaxed her hold on the knocker and waited, shivering, to be allowed entrance. Indoors, Robert slowed down his careful shuffle along the carpeted floor. He paused to switch on the light. Priscilla bustled in. She wore a long dark fur coat that matched both her boots and cossack style hat.

Laden with heavy bags, she wiped her feet before ushering him down his own hallway and back into the warm room.

'Lord, brudder, yu don know how long me been tryin to get to come an see yu. Since mi heard yu not gettin out an mi not see yu out nowhere I been mekkin promises to come. I mek miself a promise dat Christmas not gwan pass widout mi come visit yu.'

Depositing the bags on the table, she removed her coat. She continued talking while she left the room to hang the coat in the hall. On her return, she began to unpack the plastic carrier bags. She talked nonstop throughout.

'Well, brudder Robert, yu is a hard man to find. Me never see yu goin past di church dis long time. An mi keep on lookin.'

A large, round, white plastic container emerged followed by a smaller rectangular one, the lid of which showed signs of having been too near a flame. 'Mi aks and aks everybody mi see ifn dey see yu an not one body remember when dey las set dem eye pon yu. Lord, brudder Robert, mi begin to get worrid, den.'

Two more containers were placed on the table. Priscilla turned to the second bag.

'Is a good ting me a pass mi drivin test a mi could neva have dun di runnin up an down mi bin doin.' She unwrapped a teatowel from around a misshapen fruit bun. 'I went to de pastor an aks im ifn he knew anyting. Mi aks in di post office an in Michael, di butcher, cos mi know is where yu go to get yu meat.'

A round biscuit tin emerged followed by a rum bottle containing ruby red liquid.

'Den I met Mr Phillips. Yu know, Mistress Daly friend. Is her bwoyfriend really, yu know, but she jus keep on saying dey jus good friends like she is some film star or sumting. She still deny it but we all know dat she an im is more dan jus friends. True ah true.' Nodding her head while stopping to draw breath, she folded the bags neatly and placed then inside her enormous black gold-clasped patent plastic handbag. 'Mr Phillips im did tell mi dat yu hadn't bin to di club for long, long time. I aks im why smaddy din check yu out an im couldna tell mi. You know what brudder Robert? A person coulda die in dey bed an lay dere for hever in dis country. Now if it was back home, everbody would know ifn a body was ill.'

Robert wanted to remind her that the smell of the body alone would alert neighbours to a person's demise. But he couldn't get a word in. Not even when Priscilla drew breath.

'Well since me did get mi likkle car an pass me test, mi did go to di club and mi did aks dem where you was. Simple like dat.'

He speculated on the thought of Priscilla driving. She was formidable and unstoppable. Her driving instructor must have been a courageous mortal to take her on as a pupil. While the examiner, he was sure, had taken one look at her walking beside him to the car and passed her before she put the key in the ignition. Her voice and build brooked no argument. Other drivers probably avoided her at all costs. And if all else failed, she would call on her Lord and begin praying.

Robert learned from Priscilla that one of the mini bus drivers had passed on the information regarding his ill health and that she had meant to visit some time before but so many other things had got in the way.

'But why yu din come roun here an jus knock on mi door?'

'Well you know ifn yu don see smaddy these days an no one knows where dey is .... Mi din wan come knock on yu door an fin yu pass on...den mi tink dat ifn dat a happen yu children dem woulda let di church know. So at firs mi tink yu probably gone home for a vacation.' Her voice trailed off. She knew that she was offering lame excuses and contradicting her earlier statement about folks dying.

Struggling to his feet he offered her a cup of tea. He insisted that he would make it if she carried the tray in for him. While they drank tea Priscilla showed him the containers of food.

'Mi don know how yu an di family plan yu Christmas so mi bring some chicken an rice an peas an roast breadfruit. Dis is mi own cake. I put di fruit down long time since and mek di cake likkle while ago. An I jus bottle di sorrell. Yu want some now.'

She proffered the rum bottle. Together they sipped a small glass while Priscilla acknowledged the need for caution due to the liberal amount of rum she had added to her glass and the fact that she was driving.

'Mine yu, brudder, di good lawd tek care of his own.'

The afternoon drew to a close as they sat recalling Christmas 'back home.' They compared their experiences with then and now and laughed at the first few years in England. They recalled attempts to cook meals on shared cookers, then serve and eat them in your room, your only room heated by the smelly paraffin heater. They spoke of the candlewick spread covering the bed and the large 'Regentone' radiogram serving as a side board while playing music by Pauline and Roy or Johnny Ace. 'And what about those songs sung by Jim Reeves?' Or maybe you and a friend or several friends having pooled together to buy a chicken. Someone always managed to produce a bottle of white rum that 'Jus come up from home.' And always the rum would be accompanied by a story of the number of bottles they managed to get through Customs without being declared to Customs officers. And, of course, there would be the details of how that was accomplished. The rum would disappear as the card game progressed or the dominoes were slapped with feeling down on to the table.

'Lots of us spen lonely time doh, eh?'

'I remember some of dem nurses tell me dat dey spen di whole of di Chrismas in dey bed crying to go home.'

'Yes an some a dem chose to wuk because it tek dey mind of it.'

'An how dem did go to a church an not one person even bodder to say hello or Happy Christmas. An when di Pastor did speak to dem at di end of di service im eyes were as cold as di wind blowin outside and im not shakin dey han or nuttin. Is why we got our own church now, innit?'

Priscilla stayed until Sharon's key was heard in the door. Soon after that, she stood straightening the hat which, inspite of the warm room, had remained firmly on her head throughout the visit. Sister Priscilla was never seen without a hat.

Out in the hallway, she listened and clucked sympathetically while Sharon told of the preceding months with Robert. He could only hear the low murmuring of voices and he soon switched off. He therefore did not hear Sharon telling Priscilla that it would be nice if she or any of his friends could come occasionally as 'Daddy does get lonely on his own all the time. He won't admit it but he gets grumpy and short with us.'

Priscilla left. She promised to pass on the message about visits for Robert and also to return soon herself.

18

On Christmas eve, Robert and his family went to church. The suggestion came from one of his granddaughters who often accompanied her maternal grandmother to church. She asked in all innocence if the next time he went to church, could she go with him to see if it was the same as Gramma's.

'But I don go to no church darlin.'

'Daddy said that when they were little, you used to send them to church every Sunday.'

'True, true, but mi never went wid dem.'

'Then why did you make them go if you didn't go, Grandad? Gramma says that the old people should set the young ones an example.'

'Goin to church aint de only way to show hexample, young Rebecca.'

'Gramma says'.

'Rebecca for goodness sake give it a rest.' Aston, her father, smiled apologetically at Robert. 'Since she been going with Ruth's mother to that Church of God on Sundays she seems hell bent on getting everyone else there. You would think they were giving out prizes for who could swell the congregation the most. You know what happened last week, dad? Ruth and I had to go up to the school because this young lady here was almost bullying the other girls into singing hymns at play time and lunchtime. And on top of that, she was preaching to them about what would happen to their souls when they would not oblige. Apparently one of the children was so upset that she was giving her mother a hard time, refusing to go to school and all that. So the mother spoke to the head teacher who sent for us. We haven't decided what to do about Ruth's mother yet. Though this young lady here knows better than to play preacher man or woman at school again.'

Robert chuckled. 'Starting dem young, eh. She an sister Priscilla would get on fine wouldn't they?'

'Dad, it's not funny,' protested Aston. 'We have tried to explain to 'Becca that religion is a personal thing but it seems like she bound for the ministry.'

'Till she grow up and discover boys,' said Steven from the other side of the table where he was playing draughts with his son, Tyrone.

'Hush yo mout now Steven. Is fine if the chile want to go to church, but she has to learn dere is a time an place for it. She give me thought doh, dat we never all been a church together cept for you an yo brudder's weddin. An it would be nice ifn we did go on a Christmas eve.'

'Please daddy, please.' Six year old Rebecca was jumping up and down in anticipation.

'Okay. If dad thinks he can stand the car ride, we will go to the carol service on Sunday.'

Turning to his father he asked, 'What made you agree, dad?'

'I might not be here dis time nex year.'

'Oh, daddy, you musn't talk like that.' Sharon looked horrified.

'Well look at di way me a goin right now. What wid me leg an all.'

'Daddy, you are going in for a hip replacement, not a heart bypass. The doctor said that you are really quite a healthy person for your age. No blood pressure or sugar problems like so many of your contemporaries.'

'What about mi chest?'

'That's almost cleared now. You really shouldn't talk about not being here next year. Positive thinking is important if you want to get over the operation quickly. Besides, you are still young enough to lead an active life once you are fully recovered.

'Young enough to have a girlfriend anyway,' Aston added, laughing.

'Yes, dad,' enquired Steven looking up from the board. 'What happened to her? We didn't ever meet her and you never told us anything about her except that she is English.'

'Well, I not goin to start tellin you anyting in front of dese children.'

'You mean you got something you want us to know?'

'Crown me, dad. I huffed you three times, then.' Tyrone's voice rose excitedly.

'Then you must have cheated while I was talking to your grandad.'

'No, I didn't. You always say that when I beat you at anything.'

Robert was glad for the diversion that took the spotlight from him. He allowed the sound of his family to fade away as he drifted into thoughts of Doris. What was she doing now this week before Christmas? Was she thinking of him? He recalled the previous year when they had postponed seeing each other over the Christmas period after setting a date and a meeting place. 'Anyway you have my number. If you want to, you can always call me.' She never did. He recalled his emotions as the appointed date drew closer. Each time his phone rang, he anticipated that Doris would be at the other end. She wasn't. However, on the first Wednesday that they had arranged to meet, he once again caught a bus to Crystal Palace.

The French cafe at the roundabout, eleven o'clock and Doris was there waiting for him. She had been sitting close to the window. She stood and waved excitedly on his approach. He remembered clasping her hand as he lowered himself onto the cast iron chair and the whiff of lavender when she resumed her own seat. Over tea and croissants they told each other of the preceding weeks and began to plan their outings.

'Well, dad, are we definitely going to the service next Sunday then?' Aston's voice recalled him to the centre of his family.

Robert was bundled up against the chill easterly wind for his first outing in weeks. The four grandchildren argued about who was going in which car and who could sit by the window. Snowflakes were drifting down when Robert, assisted on either side by his sons, walked gingerly along the path towards the church entrance.

Sister Priscilla greeted him with a smile that split her face to reveal gleaming teeth as white as the broderie anglaise collar surrounding her neck.

'Brudder Robert, Oh Lord, brudder. Tank-yu Jesus, tank-yu Jesus.' She stepped down from where the choir were assembling and into the aisle. She ushered the family to an empty pew then sat herself down at the end beside Robert. Taking his hand, she raised her eyes to the ceiling and thanked her Lord again for bringing 'this dear friend into his house.'

The choir were already halfway through the first chorus of 'Go Tell It On The Mountain' when she rejoined them and added her voice to the rising volume of music. Robert took the opportunity to turn his head and view the congregation as the pastor rose to greet his flock.

During that first song, the number of people entering the church had swelled. Now it was filled to capacity. Full of people come to sing in Christmas day as one family in the eyes of the Lord. What a family! Old and young, some of them had with them three generations taking up several pews. Grandmothers well wrapped up against the wind that swept in each time the door opened to give entry to a latecomer. Sombre-suited grandfathers with sweaters beneath their jackets to reveal white shirts and dark ties. Mothers and fathers with their offspring sandwiched in between so as to avoid any bad behaviour. Men standing alone, women in groups almost all of them wearing hats.

'Seems mostly the women go to church dese days,' Robert mused. 'Mus be dey lookin for somting more dan de men.'

He wondered just how many of the teenagers attended regularly and how many of the smartly dressed young men had been coerced into coming by their mothers or grandmothers. There were quite a few babies held tightly in the arms of aunties and grandmothers who rocked them with vigour. They held them up fervently towards the pastor when he talked of the souls of these babies being as pure as that of the Holy Child. They halleluja-ed and amen-ed and thank-you-d Jesus with a regularity that made them seem programmed. The children clapped to the rhythm of the hymns whilst both organist and choir leader appeared to be possessed within a different world.

Robert was not the only person to remain seated when everyone rose to sing. Several older people plus a young woman in a wheelchair joined in with fervour and clapping of hands while still sitting down.

And the singing, oh the singing!

'Make a joyful noise unto the lord,' the pastor exhorted them. And that is exactly what his flock did. While they sang, Robert viewed his family. They all sang as enthusiastically as the rest.

'What would dere mudder say ifn she could see dem now? She miss all the best tings an now she missin her grans as well.'

He felt sure that Doris would have liked the singing even though he was not aware of her being a churchgoer. She sang along to all the songs that were played at the tea dance he recalled and often hummed snatches of music they heard when they were out together, particularly if there was a band playing anywhere.

'Funny how I keep tinkin of her. I wonder if she got me in her mind, too.'

The singing ended and a baby began to wail. Robert heard a voice hushing the child and could imagine the vigorous rocking that accompanied the shushing. He recalled his own childhood and the way his grandmother and aunts, all of them large ladies with ample bosoms would grab him up and clasp him so tight he could hardly breathe.

Grandmother would rock him while singing or holding a conversation with his mother. The rhythm of her rocking was very different to the tempo of the song she sang. His world heaved, rose and fell like a ship tossed in a hurricane. Closing his eyes was the only means he had then of shutting out the moving images. If he cried in protest, the arms encircling him would tighten and the motion increase even more. By the age of three, he realized that the best way for the sea to calm was to feign sleep. Unfortunately it was during this period that he often fell asleep. This was when the rhythmic motion accompanied by grandmother's humming or the drone of the aunts' voices became hypnotic and caused him to relax completely.

'Amen, Amen, Amen.' He was jerked from his reverie as the pastor's voice thundered out from the front of the church. 'Brothers and sisters, we are gathered here together to celebrate the birth of a most precious child.' He paused for breath. His eyes swept the rows before him. 'I say Amen and allelujah because before me I see faces, faces familiar and faces not so familiar. I see new faces.' Pause. 'Will I see those faces here next Sunday and the next Sunday and the Sunday after that? What is it that has brought you out on a cold dark winter's night with the snow falling? Can you truthfully say that you have come to give thanks, to celebrate, to join together at this special time?' Again he paused. The congregation were silent. The crying child was asleep. In that moment all Robert could hear were the sounds of laboured breathing from adenoidal children and chesty adults. No one murmured, 'Amen' or ,'Praise the Lord'. No feet shuffled uncomfortably on the stone floor in shoes new for Christmas. Not a sniff or a cough.

'I know and I can see those of you who come to praise the Lord often.'

Robert's eyelids grew heavy and no matter how he tried, they refused to remain open. He was a child again sandwiched between the hips of his mother on one side and those of his grandmother on the other. It was hot in the little church. His tie was choking him and his feet felt cramped enclosed in the highly polished black leather shoes. All around him the ladies vigorously waved fans or pieces of paper or shook handkerchiefs in an effort to create a breeze.

The pastor all those years ago was a white man, an Englishman who spoke of hell fire and damnation, who knew everybody's name and called them out in a thunderous voice if they dared to succumb to the arms of sleep. Even the children. Then suddenly the white Englishman was not there. In his place had been a succession of their neighbours including his own father.

His father who appeared to have swallowed a dictionary the day he was born; he never used one word when half a dozen could be spoken. Words that needed the same dictionary to interpret. Equally long were his sermons.

As he became established as one of the lay preachers it became a standing joke in the community that the rice and peas should be cooked before the family went to church because, by the time Pastor Williams finished, there would be no time left to cook. His own mother would, after some time had passed, leave her seat and walk quietly up to the pulpit and place her watch beside him.

By then Robert would be dreaming, head sunk deep onto his chest, oblivious to all including the familiar voice rising towards the wooden rafters. Many times his mother dug him sharply in his ribs or his grandmother poked the side of his head while looking straight ahead at the pulpit and murmuring, 'Amen.' Sleep always won just as it did now.

He awoke to a duet sung to a hushed audience. 'Oh Holy Night, the Stars were Brightly Shining.' Two young choir members stood alone beneath a spotlight. The rest of the church apart from the crib was in darkness. Their voices soared upwards.

'Oh night divine, oh night when Christ was born.' Rebecca slipped her hand into his. He glanced down into her shining eyes and smiled. For the first time in many, many years he prayed. Sitting in the darkened church, head bowed, while all around him faces were uplifted, ears tuned to the voices, he made a vow to himself. 'Oh Lord, if I survive the next few weeks and I am alive next Christmas, den I gwan be standin here wid Doris by my side listenin to de singin. Help me, Lord.'

19

When the day dawned that the family set off for Wales, Doris was relieved to discover that there would only be four of them in the car. Her second daughter Anne, son-in-law Martin and their son, Simon. Memories of being sandwiched between two grandchildren on the way to seaside holidays had added to her apprehension regarding the whole venture.

She had awakened early, determined to battle with Joan over travel arrangements if they were not to her satisfaction. And apart from having to sit on two sleeping bags with a pillow wedged between her and young Simon, everything seemed tolerable. Simon moaned for the first half an hour as they travelled along deserted roads in the dawn light that revealed a sky streaked with red. Huge clouds were gathering in the distance. They hung heavy and ominous, threatening rain along the journey. The thought of this did nothing to lift Doris's spirits as her grandson whined and fidgeted because he wanted to ride in one of the other cars with a cousin.

'It's going to be boring in here with only grown ups.'

'Now, Simon, stop that. You are lucky not to be crammed into Auntie Joan's car with Billy and Paula. We decided to use all of the cars, mum, including uncle Peter's estate so that we could travel in comfort.'

'Yes but there is only grown ups in here.'

'For heaven's sake! Just shut up before I turn around and take you back home to your other gran,' responded his father. 'One thing that I do not want to hear is your carrying on all the way to Wales.'

Doris wondered if he would turn around. The trouble, she thought, with most parents today was that they never carried out their threats. Small wonder they couldn't get their children to do as they were told.

For a while her thoughts meandered back to when she and Frank were raising their four children. He was the disciplinarian, believing that children obey immediately. Good training, he called it. Helped him cope with military life. Mind you, she always agreed with what he said and when she did have the occasion to reprimand one of the children herself if he were out, then she maintained her stand about going to bed early, no jam on bread, or cake for tea, and ultimately getting a taste of her slipper.

Somewhere along the way, over the years, times and attitudes had changed. Even her own children were not as firm as she and Frank had been. Her grandchildren weren't too bad really. Some of her friends at the club told such horror stories about theirs. Her head sank lower as the car crossed over Hammersmith Bridge and headed towards the M4 motorway. Rain was falling and the windscreen wipers squeaked rhythmically as they swept hypnotically backwards and forwards across the glass.

Simon's petulant voice faded. The sound of a carol sung by Nat (King) Cole on the radio, accompanied by Anne and Martin singing along was the last thing Doris heard until the little convoy stopped at a service station for breakfast.

The rain continued throughout the day. Not a glimmer of sunlight could be seen through the dark, low clouds. The beam from the headlights of the cars illuminated sheets of spray, flung by the huge lorries thundering past, across the windscreens of slow moving cars. In the stops between, everyone dashed through puddles across pitted asphalt car parks to arrive inside breathless and damp, and sit steaming at plastic covered tables to drink yet more tea or coffee. Doris and Simon dozed after lunch, eaten in a place where carols were belted out of speakers at a deafening rate of decibels. And the tepid tea resembled dishwater. Afterwards in the car, she played 'I spy' with Simon until he gave up and asked for a different game, during which they both fell asleep again. They both missed the crossing over the Severn Bridge and, also, a pile up of several cars that had collided into the back of a juggernaut.

Darkness had fallen when they finally reached the cottage. Welcoming lights shone through the windows. A huge fire blazed in the hearth.

'Thank goodness for that,' breathed Joan as she signed a slip of paper and relieved the owner of the keys. Doris offered to make tea while the other adults and Billy unloaded the cars. The three younger children ran screaming and shouting from room to room until Peter yelled at them to 'either sit down, or help, instead of getting under everyone's feet.'

A long wooden table stood in the middle of the huge bright, neon lit kitchen. The cooking range ran along one end with pots and pans hung from above on butcher's hooks. There were two kettles. One electric, white and sterile sitting at the back of the fitted unit. The other a pot-bellied aluminium one was on the range, already hot. Doris was reminded of her mother's kitchen when she saw the kettle and the large pale green, enamel teapot beside it.

Eventually the cars were empty. Wet coats dripped steadily where they were hung in a row from pegs beside the door. Sodden shoes steamed before the fire. Everyone sat at the table clasping a mug of hot tea and munching on ginger biscuits. Even the children were quiet. A moment of contentment, thought Doris. If only it would last.

Though the bedroom assigned to her was quite small, Doris said nothing when her daughter showed her into it later that night. Grateful for having a space to herself, she wished her family goodnight soon after and retired to unpack her clothes and the gifts she would be giving the next day. The narrow bed tucked against the wall proved to be more comfortable than she expected and it wasn't long before she fell into a dead sleep.

She awoke in the early hours of the morning to an uncanny silence. The room was pitch black or so it seemed. Several minutes passed before her eyes adjusted and she realized where she was.

Doris was thoroughly used to the sound of London traffic trundling past her house during most hours of the day and night. There were nights when she lay, reading or trying to sleep. Voices, sometimes raucous, sometimes angry, most often very loud, would penetrate the double glazing and heavy curtaining of her bedroom window causing her to sigh or mutter to herself. On the odd occasion an argument rumbled on and on, flaring up into incoherent shouting or screaming. Then it would all die down to a murmur that persisted, invading her peace and preventing her from falling asleep.

She would waken suddenly, eyes wide in the darkness but know immediately where she was, surprised that she had eventually slept. When this happened, Doris often found it difficult to sleep again. Frustrated with trying, she would pad across to the bathroom then downstairs to make a cup of tea while grumbling to herself about the inconsiderate nature of people who were probably enjoying making up, wrapped in each other's arms after the quarrel. While she would most probably be awake for hours. Quite often when she returned to her bed, Doris found her thoughts drifting towards Robert.

Since losing contact, her waking time during the night was dominated by him and the time they spent together. Now, as usual, her mind travelled that path as she lay wide-eyed in the darkness. Left behind in her wardrobe was a pair of black leather gloves and a book of 'green London' walks. Not wrapped or labelled. Bought and hidden away just in case he might make contact. What would they have been doing during the past few weeks especially with all the rain there had been, she wondered. And how would they have prepared for Christmas?

Scenarios floated before her where she lay, quilt up to her chin, arms crossed covering her breasts, with her hands smoothing each shoulder in a caressing motion. A special lunch in a local carvery, sitting across from each other at a table for two. An open fire where logs crackled and spat. On the table was a simple decoration wreathing a red candle. The fire reflected in Robert's eyes while she could feel her cheeks glowing from its heat or her feelings for him. She speculated on going with Robert to his club for a Caribbean celebration. Even though the food provided was similar to English Christmas fare, she savoured the many flavours that she had developed a taste for on their picnics. Then there was the prospect of sharing a meal with him in his own home. Perhaps with him and his family or even, probably, just the two of them.

Doris's hands stilled. Turning on to her side, she drew her knees up. Both hands were now pillowing her cheek. Christmas dinner with him. She imagined him holding out the chair for her to sit at a carefully laid table. His gentle hands would unfold a napkin and lay it across her lap. Then dish by dish, the food carried in and placed in front of her before he sat down himself. Background music playing and lights twinkling on a small tree in the corner under which she had put her gift to him. After dinner, after dinner. What about after dinner? Turning again, Doris closed her eyes trying to block out the scenes that seemed to be projected onto the dark wall opposite. His family arriving. Eating at her house and her family arriving. Robert accepting an invitation from her to eat in her home. She and Robert sitting together on a settee listening to music. In her house or his? How would the good-byes be said? Goodbye. There may not be any transport. Taxies cost double. His house or hers? No. That could never be, could not happen, would not happen. Because we are both too old. Because our families would not approve. Because he is black and I am white. Because I would not dare. Take your pick, Doris. She found herself hugging the pillow. Because I don't know where you are. How I wish I did. In the darkness of the tiny room she heard a voice whispering, 'Robert, oh Robert, where are you.'

Despite being awake during the night, Doris was the first one of the family to stir. None of the children appeared when, after leaving the bathroom she proceeded to make herself a cup of coffee in the still warm kitchen. Sitting at the table chewing thoughtfully on a left over ginger biscuit, hands cupped around the mug, she told herself sternly to put Robert out of her mind until she returned home. Then and only then could she concentrate on finding him again.

In contrast to her bedroom, the kitchen was comfortably noisy. The range clicked each time the fuel gauge adjusted itself.

The kettle continued to hiss as it cooled while the clock ticked itself towards Christmas day. She drew back the curtain and opened the venetian blind. It was still dark outside though the distant sky was red streaked with black. The rain must have stopped during the night, she thought, because the outside of the windows were dry. At least the children will be able to get out during the day if they wrap up well. I really don't want to be cooped up in here for the next three days with everybody. She wondered why she had agreed to come anyway. But she knew the answer: you are here because you needed to take your mind off him. Her eyes clouded as her dreams from the darkness returned.

Before she managed to drain the mug, Doris heard the sounds of her grandchildren discovering their gift-filled stockings. The next two hours were noisy with activity which bordered on frenetic. While the children alternately argued with each other over the contents of their stockings, asked for a present, or complained of being hungry, the adults attempted to placate or reason with them. They used the bathrooms, made each other cups of coffee or decided who wanted what for breakfast. Silence descended momentarily when breakfast commenced.

The children sat perched on stools at the breakfast bar spooning cereal with hot milk into their mouths. The adults sat contentedly around the table. The aroma of freshly toasted bread mingled with grilled bacon and coffee added to the ambience.

Soon Joan was delegating her family to their various tasks. The children were sent to watch a film on the television in order that dinner could be prepared and they were promised a further gift once the work was done. Doris, having refused to be included with the juveniles, remained at the table doing minor tasks that were offered her.

She grudgingly admitted that her bossy daughter's organizational skills had paid off. She produced tightly sealed plastic bags of previously prepared vegetables. Recently thawed sausages wrapped in slices of ham accompanied a magnificent turkey and a spiced beef joint was put into the oven. Pudding, mince pies and cream appeared as did the almost completed sherry trifle which Doris then undertook to decorate.

When preparations were completed to her satisfaction, Joan announced that after a well earned drink of 'whatever you fancy,' she thought the men could take the children out for a walk while anyone who stayed behind could set up a treasure hunt for them. 'What do you want to do, mum?' Doris felt an hour's sleep might be good for her, except she did not want to be on her own with her thoughts. It seemed to her that every waking moment she allowed herself to detach from the bustle of the family, Robert came to mind. If she kept herself busy and within the group she might not think about him.

'I'll have a glass of sherry and offer ideas for the treasure hunt from a chair, I think.'

Sitting and adding her comments as to where prizes might be hidden or clues left did not offer as much of a distraction for Doris as she had hoped. If she was a superstitious person Doris would have been convinced by now that Robert was haunting her or trying to reach out to her from wherever he was.

And for every thought that entered her mind, a question arose regarding her family or his. She was relieved when the rest of her family returned red-cheeked and bright-eyed from the wind. They burst into the kitchen requesting hot drinks and food. Positioning herself behind the breakfast bar, Doris provided everyone with their choice of beverage. Mince pies and chocolates were dispensed before the treasure hunt began.

Suddenly the day was over. The sky darkened. Blinds and curtains were drawn and everyone found somewhere comfortable to sit in the spacious sitting room while the final preparations were made to the dinner. They managed to complete dinner without an argument breaking out between the children over the contents of a cracker. They began to reminisce.

Doris listened. She nodded when her children told of past Christmases, of the things their father had done or said. She added memories that they omitted along with some about her own childhood. And she raised her glass to sip the wine each time there was a lull in the conversation. Perhaps it was the wine, or the fact that she felt a little tired. A feeling of melancholia swept over her which to her horror was not linked with memories of her late husband but with a sense of loneliness and a longing for Robert that consumed her when she realized she did not have a partner with her.

'Another drink, mum?'

'Think I will. Thank you.'

The conversation flowed around the table, adult to adult, adult to child, child to adult, child to child. At times everyone was talking at once and the noise was almost unbearable. When the noise died down a little, the opportunities to pass food or drink were taken up and the conversation resumed.

The family moved back to the space around the fire while the dishwasher was loaded with the empty plates and utensils. Standing up to walk across the room Doris felt a little woozy. She steadied herself against the back of the settee, then carefully placing one foot after the other walked to the chair she had previously occupied.

Two glasses of sherry later she made her apologies and attempted to rise, saying that she was extremely tired and was going to bed. Her head was spinning. She needed something solid to hold on to if she was going to make it to her room. Tottering slightly she tried again to navigate the room.

'Here we go round the roundabouts,' she giggled. Peter took her arm.

'Mum I think you have had one sherry too many this evening. Let me give you a hand.' At the door of her room she thanked him and assured him she could manage from there. Yet her voice was coming from far away, sounding giggly and girlish. She felt as if she had just stepped down from a fairground merry go round.

'I need to lie down.'

She spoke aloud to herself as the door closed and the carpeted floor rose to meet her like waves billowing across a seashore.

Doris was dreaming. She stood in the centre of a roundabout that was bright with summer flowers. The surrounding road was filled with heavy traffic that caused the earth to vibrate beneath her feet. The noise filled her head punctuated by the horns and hooters of irate drivers. Looking across the road she could see

Robert leaning on his stick waiting for the flow of traffic to cease in order to allow him to cross the crossing. Someone was calling her, 'Doris, Doris come on. Get down from there and cross to me.' It sounded like Frank. Turning her head towards the shops, she could just make him out. He was waving a black leather glove. 'Here. I'm over here.'

'But I...'

She turned again, this time towards the park. The crossing was empty of people as traffic trundled over. 'Doris, here, Doris.' She looked towards The Sportsman public house. There he was. Lifting her arm to wave and to call his name, her view was obscured by an extraordinarily long juggernaut roaring by. It turned onto Church road. Stepping carefully over the lilies and asters, Doris tried to cross the roundabout, her eyes anxiously scanning the road opposite for Robert. He was not there.

'Oh dear. Oh, wait, please wait,' she called as she saw him enter the wrought iron entrance gates to the park. 'Wait for me. I want to come with you, Robert.'

Another, more persistent voice was calling, calling insistently. She heard an urgent knocking. It pierced the turbulence of her dream causing her to surface from the smell of fumes mingled with the scent of lilies and the roar of the traffic.

'Nan, Nan, are you okay? Nan, I made you a coffee.'

Doris struggled to extract herself from the twisted duvet and the dream. Sitting up in the grey half light she called to Billy to come in.

'Wow, Nan, I've been knocking for ages. Thought you were dead or something.'

'Well I'm certainly not dead. So what do you suggest the something might be?'

Billy placed the mug he was carrying on the bedside table and sat down on the bed beside her. Grinning, he turned and said, 'Dead drunk more like, Nan.'

'No, never. I wasn't.'

'Oh, yes, you were! You should have seen yourself.'

'Get away Billy. I've never been drunk in my life.'

The mischief in his eyes was missed by Doris when she leant to pick up the mug.

'You were singing and dancing and staggering everywhere. Mum was not amused.'

'I don't believe you, you scallywag, you. I hardly had a drink. Oh no!'

She recalled the first sherry and the glass that was topped up several times during the afternoon and then the wine in the evening. 'Surely not.'

'Gosh, Nan, you should see your face. You weren't really that bad but you were tiddly, honest. Uncle Peter helped you walk across the room. You kept saying something about going round the roundabouts. We thought you meant merry go rounds.'

'What time is it?'

'Eleven thirty!'

'What I need is some food and a walk in the fresh air to clear my head.'

'You got a hangover, Nan?'

'Go away, young man. And let me pull myself together.'

Billy backed out of the room parodying a drunkard trying to walk a straight line.

After a breakfast of cereal followed by toast and marmalade prepared by Billy, Doris prepared to take a brisk walk. She pulled on her boots, coat and accessories. She wanted to walk alone but gave in to the chorus of protestations that rose as she announced her intention. Instead, she walked accompanied by her grandchildren. They were all eager to get away from the warnings and threats of their parents.

Billy walked beside her while the others alternately ran or skipped along the narrow lane. Half a mile from the cottage they turned left onto a muddy path leading down to the sea shore. Billy gave her his hand as they negotiated the ruts and stones. His cousins and sister continued at breakneck speed down the path and were already leaping and squealing along the sand and over pools when she reached the bottom.

The biting wind caused her to pull her woollen hat further down over her ears and adjust the collar of her coat. Thrusting her hands deep into the pockets, she trudged along. The shrieks of the children were mingled with the screams of the gulls as they wheeled and turned swooping down onto the white crested waves where they bobbed for a while before taking flight again. Occasionally one of the children returned, outstretched hand towards her, showing her a shell or a pebble. Then away they went, running and jumping, calling to the others to wait.

'Go on, Billy, I'm fine walking along here. Go with the others if you want to.'

'You sure, Nan?' Already he was edging away from her half turned, bent forward, looking first at her then the other children.

'Yes, go on. Not too far, mind you. And it's safer if you're close to the younger ones anyway.'

He needed no urging and leapt away with a hoarse shout peculiar to adolescent boys whose voices range from octave to octave.

Doris recalled her recent conversation with Amy as they travelled towards Herne Hill on their way to visit a friend who had not been able to attend the lunch club.

'What's wrong, Doris?

'Nothing. Why?'

'I wouldn't be asking if I didn't know you as well as I do.'

'I'm alright, Amy. Honestly, I am.'

Amy was undeterred. 'You have been, well, a bit off. Distant, preoccupied. It's difficult to explain, Doris. Have I done something to upset you? Are you ill?'

Doris could not remember the last time anyone had inquired after her health and well being. The familiar choking feeling welled up. Not for the first time, she felt close to tears.

'Come on, Doris, I'm your friend, remember?' Amy patted her hand. 'Tell me what it is.'

Doris sighed, wondering where to begin and how much she should say.

'Remember when I won those tickets for the tea dance and you got upset because I didn't invite you to accompany me?'

'Mmm.'

Doris rubbed the side of her face. She drew her hand across her mouth before she continued. 'Well, I have this friend. Or, had this friend. A man friend. I've been seeing him every week for about eighteen months. On a Wednesday.'

'You've got a boyfriend, Doris?'

'Not a boy friend, actually. He's just a bit older than me.'

'I didn't mean a toyboy, Doris. What's his name? What's he like?'

'His name's Robert. He is very kind and he's a real gentleman, polite and kind. But, I haven't seen him for a while and I don't know how to get in contact or anything.'

'Where does he live? Haven't you got his telephone number?' Realising that the bus had stopped, Amy glanced up. 'Come on, we're there. You can tell me while we walk.' She linked arms with Doris and continued, 'If you have his number, all you have to do is ring it!'

'It isn't as simple as that, Amy. We always made arrangements to meet at the same place, same time, same day. Wednesday.'

'Sounds a bit like Brief Encounters to me, Doris Thomas,' interrupted Amy, ever the humorist. 'Is he tall, dark and handsome?'

'No, he's not tall or particularly handsome but he is, anyway, after the tea dance I went back to the cafe several times and waited for ages. He never came.'

'Perhaps he didn't want to continue seeing you.'

Amy pulled away from her friend.

'How could you say such a thing when you've never met him?'

She stood still glaring at her.

'Come on, Doris. We've been friends too long for us to fall out over a man, eh?'

Amy took her arm and gently propelled her towards the kerb where they paused before crossing the road. 'Have you done anything at all about trying to find him?'

'Apart from waiting at the cafe and asking directory enquiries. I can't think of anything else to do.'

'No luck with the telephone, then?'

'I didn't have an address.'

Arm in arm they turned the corner and began to walk up the slight incline of Redpost Hill.

'Doesn't he have your number, Doris?'

'That's what's so stupid. I never gave him mine.'

'Why not?'

'I don't know really.'

'If you like him as much as I think you do, Doris, you were silly not to give him yours. You do like him, don't you?'

'Oh yes, yes I do. And I wish I could contact him. I've lain awake at night trying to remember if he actually said which road he lived on. I've racked my brains for a way to find him. You see, he was waiting for a hip replacement operation.' She paused.

'Well?'

'He mentioned someone called Priscilla. I rather got the impression that she was sort of pursuing him.'

'Did he say she was? Did he tell you what he thought about it?'

'I think he was amused by her.'

'Humph. That doesn't sound like much of threat if you ask me, unless they were more than just good friends.'

'No, I don't think so.'

Amy interrupted again, 'And what about you and him Doris? Were you?'

'Were we what Amy?'

'Alright then if you weren't, would you?'

'Let's just say I have given it some serious thought lately.'

'All this time Doris and you never let on. Did you think I would steal him?'

'I wouldn't put anything past you, Amy Fitzpatrick.'

'He's that nice, is he?'

'He certainly is.'

They giggled as they stopped before the cast iron gates of a large house.

'You know, Doris, it could be because of the weather. We have had a lot of frost this winter and it has been quite treacherous. But, it is improving, now. Maybe he'll turn up soon.'

The children in the distance, Doris walked now buffeted by the wind. She listened to the waves crashing on the shore. She considered the previous night. She remembered the meal prior to retiring to her room. Then she had given in to tiredness while admitting to herself that she must certainly have drunk a little more than she should have done. All she could remember now was that both Frank and Robert figured in her dream.

20

Sharon prepared to take her father into hospital on the appointed day. Robert's bag had been packed the previous evening when the family gathered to wish him well and to double-check the final arrangements for post operative visits. The nightshirts were folded in with towels and shaving equipment, talcum powder, soap, tissues, fruit juice and several books. All that was left to be done was to telephone the hospital as requested to confirm his admittance that day.

At eight thirty the telephone rang. Robert limped from the kitchen to answer it before Sharon, who was stripping the sheets from his bed, could pick it up. She entered the room to hear her father arguing with the person at the other end.

'What you mean, I can't come in today? I been waiting here in dis house for months to get me leg fixed. Don't tell me bout no odder people needing mi bed. I need di bed. I need to get mi leg done.'

Sharon took the receiver from his hand. 'Hello, I'm Mr Williams' daughter. Is there a problem?'

He watched her face as she listened in silence. He could hear the female voice at the other end explaining that there was a shortage of beds due to a spate of emergencies. People slipping on the frost. 'On top that, we are very short-staffed as quite a few of the nurses are down with a bug, flu or something.'

'Can you tell me just how long it will be before my father can be admitted? What do you mean you can't say? He is in considerable pain. And now for the first time in weeks, he is actually clear of any infection. I know you can't help it. Listen, what excuse would you have if you were making this call in midsummer, I'd like to know.' She returned the receiver and turning to her father, she smiled apologetically. 'Looks like you are going to have to wait at least a couple of weeks. According to her, they'll telephone you as soon as there is a bed available. Meanwhile, there is nothing they can do. Look, daddy, why don't you let me and the boys pay?'

'No. I tole you already that I done paid my dues an I entitle to a bed in de hospital.'

'Surely the pain you are in.'

'I'll manage wid de painkillers de doctor give me. When it get too bad, maybe.' His voice trailed off. Something in his head was reminding him that the longer it was before he entered hospital, the longer the delay before finding Doris.

Lying in bed each night during the Christmas holiday, he had planned that as soon as he was able and the weather permitted, he would return to the Palace. Every single Wednesday he would go and sit in the cafe on the parade and watch out for her. Surely if she cared for him and wanted to see him again she would come to look for him at the old rendezvous. If that didn't work, he planned to travel down to Paxton roundabout and wait at the bus stop. He would do it every morning if need be. She must come to the bus stop when she was going to the hairdressers. That's it. He could save himself a lot of trouble. All he had to do was go in there and enquire about her. He could leave a message in there. Just a small problem. What would the staff in the salon think? How would Doris react when the hairdresser told her that an old black man had been in asking for her. She might be embarrassed. And just supposing she didn't want to see him anymore. No, she must feel something for me. She let me kiss her and she kiss me back, he decided.

Three more weeks passed. Weeks when he willed the telephone to ring and for Doris to be on the end of the line. Weeks when he planned and plotted various ways that he could contact her again. Frost and occasional snow prevented him from venturing outside unless one of the children took him from the door to the car in preparation for a journey to the shops or their respective homes.

In early February he developed another chest infection and was confined to bed for several days with a high temperature under threat of hospitalization if it didn't improve.

'I suppose that's one way of getting a bed,' Steven told his elder brother when he called New York to tell him. 'Problem is it wouldn't be on an orthopaedic ward. He would go onto a geriatric ward and probably die before his leg was done.'

While he was in bed, Sister Priscilla called regularly with nourishing soup, heavy with dumplings and ground provision.

'You eat up all dat yam and breadfruit an stuff, brudder Robert. You got to get strong an healthy ready for yu operation, yu know.'

She had made cornmeal porridge sweetened with lashings of condensed milk. And she left him jugs of Guinness punch to drink. 'I want to see yu up an runnin nex time me come.'

His reports of her visits amused Sharon and her brothers. They were convinced that Priscilla had her sights set on him alone.

'Give her half a chance and she'd be giving me a bed bath an all,' he grumbled. 'Telling me if I sit out on de chair she will change de sheets on me bed. Me tell her you do dat for me, Sharon, and dere's no need for she to bodder sheself.'

'Why don't you give her a chance, dad? She must be looking for a husband and it appears you are the one for her.'

'She alright,' he conceded. 'But she not for me.'

'I got my plans for when my leg done.'

Sharon tucked a blanket around his knees and moved the table with the telephone nearer to his chair.

'Daddy, you are so, so secretive. You keep everything to yourself. If only you'd share your worries with us.'

'Me ever do dat yet? Is not your place to know me business.'

'I don't want to know your business, daddy. I want to know what it is that keeps you down.'

'Nuttin keepin me down.'

'The only time I hear you laugh is when you and Sister Priscilla sit here going over old times. And even then I get the feeling that you holding back.'

'What yu mean?'

'Well,' she paused, and held her breath. The sound of the clock and the soft hiss of the gas fire intermingled with Robert's heavy breathing.

'You have this old fashioned idea, that because we are your children, we are only supposed to know what you consider concerns us. We scarcely know anything about your life before you came to England, or come to think of it, since you've been here. We really don't know anything about what you do, or did with yourself every day. And you never talk about our mother.'

'Yu leave dat woman out of it, aint none of your business.'

'You see what I mean, everything is 'none of our business'. Yet here we are taking care of you, worrying about you, trying our best to cheer you up. And you sit there with your long face, staring into nowhere, sighing as if you have the weight of the whole world on your shoulders, refusing to let us in.' She told herself that she had gone this far and that she might just as well finish. 'Why is knowing about our mother none of our business? What did she do that was so bad? The boys say that all they can remember is that she was here one day and gone the next. Is it thoughts of her that make you miserable?'

'Phew,' Sharon told her brothers later, 'I couldn't believe what I'd said. It was like a dam bursting. Once I started I couldn't stop.'

'And what was his reaction?' asked Aston.

'He didn't speak for ages. Just sat there looking at me, you know the way he used to when we were naughty. Then he sort of slumped in the chair looking really sad.'

'And you, what did you do?' interrupted Steven.

'I think I held my breath. Then he told me how he hated being dependent on us and how he wished he could get out and about because, now don't either of you dare say anything to him about this. He was still seeing that friend of his, you know, the one who never turned up for dinner that time. He hasn't been able to contact her. Apparently he gave her his telephone number but she has not called him. He feels that somehow he has let her down. You know what fellas? I think our dad is quite fond of this mysterious woman.'

'Is there anything we can do to get in touch with her for him?'

'No. He was adamant about that. Said that after his op, he knew where to go to look for her. Stubborn old man.'

'And what did he tell you about mum?'

'Nothing, nothing at all. He refused to be drawn into that.'

February twenty-ninth dawned with a clear blue sky. Everywhere was covered with a sparkling frost, so thick it resembled snow. Robert stood at the window, leaning heavily on his stick, looking at his garden. He coughed again and again trying to clear the mucus that had gathered overnight and caused his chest to feel tight and uncomfortable. The coughing not only made him dizzy but gave him a dull ache in the back of his neck and across his shoulders.

'Lord,' he groaned. 'Can anybody see mi trial?'

Taking a deep breath, he turned towards the kitchen door intending to make himself a mug of hot lemon and honey. Carefully, reaching for the back of his chair, he leant for extra support on the stick. One more step and he could hold on to the door. He put out his hand. His body was shaken by a paroxysm of coughing.

'Oh mi gawd!' He gasped as the carpet came up to meet him and the room swam round and round.

Desperately trying to steady himself, he felt in the air for the door again. Then he fell. Arms flailing helplessly in the air, his legs gave way and he crashed onto the carpet. His head caught the edge of the door. His leg twisted beneath him. The pain in his hip was indescribable. He lay wedged between the door and the dresser. The upturned chair rested on top of him. Mercifully, he passed out.

Throughout the day, he drifted in and out of consciousness. He tried to drag his body from beneath the chair but the intense pain in his leg made him cry out and freeze. His head hurt. When he reached with his hand to feel the sore place that nagged at him, the area was sticky. Blood no longer oozed from his head. He called weakly, knowing it was in vain because his neighbour was out at work.

Each attempt to move resulted in excruciating pain. He could only judge the time by the depth of light in the room whenever he surfaced from semi-consciousness. Although the heating was on, he began to feel the cold creeping into his stiff limbs. To his shame, during the afternoon a liquid warmth spread beneath him. His eyes filled with tears. Pain and frustration at his inability to help himself made him try repeatedly to move, only to be rendered immobile by the fire that pervaded his body. Darkness fell. He lay inert, numb, his stiff body pinned by the chair. When he was conscious, he was confused. He mumbled incoherently into the heavy blackness surrounding him.

He did not hear Sharon's key or her voice calling from the hallway. When light flooded the room, he was in Jamaica swimming in the Caribbean sea towards Doris who sat mermaid fashion on a reef calling him, calling him and waving her pink plump arms.

'Here I am, Robert. Over here, dear. Robert, can you see me?'

21

For almost three weeks Robert gave cause for concern. Following an operation to pin the fractured femur and replace his hip, he developed pneumonia. The injury to his head healed quickly but he was confused and disorientated appearing to think he was in the Caribbean swimming to catch up with someone. No amount of reassurance from his family could ease the agitated state he was in. The doctors eventually decided to keep him mildly sedated.

He was a difficult patient, continually trying to remove tubing in order to get out of bed. He grumbled when nurses were attending to his needs and complained when he was left alone. Sharon and her brothers were dismayed. Although they were aware of his independent attitude it hadn't occurred to them that he would give such aggravation to the people looking after him. A consultant for geriatric medicine visited him along with a psychiatrist who specialized in the same field. Following a family conference, it was decided that once he was physically healed, Robert would need round the clock supervision and care if his mental state showed no sign of improving. Initially he would go onto a geriatric ward until the social workers were able to find suitable accommodation. His children were horrified. Devon flew over from New York hoping that by seeing his son again, Robert would settle down.

There was a slight improvement. During the time his eldest son visited, Robert allowed the physiotherapist to get him out of bed and manipulate his damaged leg. When everyone else admired his nightshirts and commented on how sensible they were, he rumbled on about his private parts not being private and insisted that as soon as his operation site was healed he would be wearing pyjama bottoms. He took his medication and was generally less demanding. The chest infection began to subside. The daily battle to keep an oxygen mask on his face was no longer a necessity. To the relief of everyone he began to eat. Yet, he continued to appear depressed and no matter what the family tried or suggested, he did not respond. As his behaviour improved, the nurses no longer regarded him as a troublesome old man. Instead they were sympathetic to his depression and tried numerous ways of cheering him up.

'Sister will be back from her holiday soon and she will have you running up and down here as if you were training for the marathon, Mr Williams. If I were you, I would make sure that I was well enough to be discharged before she got back.'

'Where she gone, then? I been here a long time an I haven't seen her.'

'She saved up all her leave this year and went home to Jamaica for eight weeks. She is due back at the end of the month.'

'Is how long I been here?'

'Nearly six weeks.'

'No!'

'Yes. You were in quite a state when you came up from Casualty. Thought we were going to lose you.'

'Well me knew it was a long time but me never realize it that long. What hospital me in?'

The nurse told him.

'Why me not inna mi local hospital?'

'The night you were brought in, there were no beds in your local one.'

'An me had to bruk me leg in order fi dem to fix me bad hip, eh.'

She shrugged. 'Now try and stand up while I straighten these cushions behind you. Lean on the frame. That's it.'

The nurse completed her ministrations and left Robert to his thoughts. He was roused from them by the arrival of Priscilla.

'Lord, brudder Robert, is so long me been tryin fi get to see yu.'

She planted a large plastic carrier bag on the table straddling the foot of his bed. Then removing her fur coat to reveal a green striped suit fastened with the most enormous gilt buttons, she dragged a chair across the floor, dusted the seat with a tissue and seated herself. Almost without pausing for breath, she continued, 'I kep on ringing yu childrens and dey tole me yu was really ill. Dat it was bes ifn yu dint have any visits. I jus ring Sharon once a week so dat I could tell di pastor an alla dem how yu was doin. We pray for yu, yu know, brudder Robert.'

Before he could open his mouth, Sister Priscilla stood up. She closed her eyes, lifted her hands towards the ceiling and in her loudest pulpit voice proceeded to bring the routine of the entire ward to a halt.

'Lord Jesus, oh Lord Jesus,' she entreated. 'Tank yu lord fi bringin our dear brudder safe trew di fire.' Robert shrank in his chair. He covered his face, not to join in the prayer, but to hide his embarrassment. Priscilla's voice carried out of the small side room that he occupied, to every corner of the ward, including the bathrooms. Staff and patients alike turned to see where the voice was coming from.

'No wonder he has been confused if he's been trying to prevent her from coming in and embarrassing him like that,' said the nurse who had earlier been attending to him.

'How do you know he isn't joining with her?' replied a colleague.

'I've just looked through the window. He is covering his face.'

The praying continued for a full five minutes during which time the unwilling listeners themselves prayed for the ritual to cease.

'Amen, amen.'

'And amen, again,' muttered the staff nurse as at last Priscilla sat down. She then proceeded to decant from her bag what seemed to Robert to be enough food for the whole ward.

'Me know you mus be missin real food, so mi bring yu groun provision and ting to build up yu strength.' The plastic dishes and containers were laid out along the bed. 'Jus aks de nurses dem to heat it up a likkle in de microwave when yu is ready fi eat. Now tell me truly, brudder Robert, how is yu doin?'

Priscilla stayed for an hour. During this time she gave orders for a nurse to remove all the food from the bed, to label the containers and put them in the ward kitchen fridge. It was no use telling her that it was against the rules. She gave Robert news of church members and happenings. She exhorted him to get well soon. Finally, she stood up and donned her coat. 'I will be back nex week, me deah,' she said patting him on the arm. 'Mine yu eat up all o de provisions I brung yu. An I will bring some more when me come.'

A hush descended on the ward while patients and staff alike drew breath before resuming normal life again.

The nurses continued to tease Robert until they went off duty. They passed on the afternoon's entertainment to the next shift coming on duty.

Unknown to Priscilla, she had provided an impetus to the healing process for Robert. The interest that the nurses developed and the manner of their teasing helped to humour Robert. He began to respond mentally and physically. The scar on his forehead was already fading and he had begun to take short trips up and down the main ward to which he had been moved.

But within days he developed a secondary infection in the leg wound and was transferred back into a side room shortly before the regular ward sister returned from her leave. He ran a temperature. He felt lethargic and during the previous night, he had been confused again. He insisted that he was trying to swim to the rock on which Doris was waiting for him.

On the second day of his isolation he lay in bed covered only by a sheet. A table top fan blew cooling air over him. His eyes were closed when he heard a voice he thought he recognized out side the slightly open door.

'Mr Robert Williams. I remember taking that telephone call about him just as I was going off duty before my leave.' There was something familiar about the woman that caused him to open his eyes. 'How come he is still here? We don't usually keep hips this long.'

Another voice responded to give her his history before she opened the door fully and came across the room. He kept his eyes closed trying to recall where he had heard the voice before. He waited to hear it again.

'Robert? Hello, Robert, Mr Williams.'

He did not open his eyes.

'I'll come back later. He's sleeping now, nurse. How often are you doing his observations?'

He opened his eyes and saw the long straight back moving towards the door. No mop and bucket now. No striped dress or protective apron. She wore a navy dress with a tight black elastic belt. Her hands held his file.

'Is you?'

The woman in the navy blue dress turned.

'So many years pass yu forget what I look like?'

How many years and she don't look no older, thought Robert.

She stood speechless, her mouth slightly open, her eyes wide. Turning, she told the nurse she would be with her in a moment. Now she stood over him.

'Such a common name. I stopped looking carefully at the files of Robert Williams years ago.'

Sitting down on the chair beside his bed, she leaned forward as if to get a closer look.

'Me look a lot older dan yu, eh?'

Silence.

'I don't know what to say.' Her voice was hoarse.

'Look, just let me finish the ward round and I will be back.' She patted the bed. Not his hand but the space between his body and his wrist. He watched the straight back exit from the little room as the memories of his first encounter came flooding back. He waited.

He realised that he'd been waiting a very long time. Was there anything he wanted to say to her? All those years, the long nights when he lay awake wondering what she was doing, where she was, how she could have left her children, what else could he have done to keep her. She never even asked me, told me what she was planning. I wouldn't have stopped her. Instead she left.

About an hour later she came in and carefully closed the door behind her. Sitting down, she waited silently. Her hands were folded neatly in her lap. Her back was ramrod straight.

'Robert.'

'Why?'

Silence again.

'Yu not sorry yu went?'

'I had to. I was suffocating. More than anything in the world I wanted to train to be a nurse.'

'An yu tink I woulda stopped yu?'

'Not just you, Robert. It was everything. Everything.'

'Where yu went to?'

'I applied to a hospital in Birmingham to train as a State Registered Nurse. When I got there I realized they were directing me towards training as a State Enrolled Nurse. I stayed there three months while I applied to some other hospitals. It took all that time.' She talked of when she went for the last interview, how she was so angry that she told them what she thought of the system. She asked them what right they had to keep putting 'us onto inferior training courses. Most of us had recceived an education as good as theirs and we were in England by invitation of Mr Enoch Powell.' She warmed to the subject. 'He came to Jamaica when he was the Minister of Health and told us at our school, my school, how short of nurses English hospitals were. So, I told them that if I wanted to scrub floors and clean up behind people, I could have stayed home and been a maid.' When she finished, the matron looked at her and looked at her papers and the test she had just been made to do. And she didn't speak for ages. She kept looking over her glasses at her. 'Then she said, and I never forget this, 'Well, young lady, you have made your point. You have enough anger in you to fire a hundred hospital boilers. If I take you into this hospital to train as a registered nurse, you must give me an undertaking to keep that fire dampened down. I do not take lightly to my nurses losing their tempers. Let this be the one and only time.'

'I just sat there Robert. Never realized she was giving me a place in the training school. Not till she asked me if I had my bags with me because she would get the Home Sister to show me my room in the nurses' home. I was the only black nurse in that hospital. But I finished and did staff nurse there for two years before I moved on.'

'Yu was always on fire, always angry now dat I tink of it. From de firs time me did set mi eyes pon yu wid yu mop an bucket, swishin up di corridor.'

'You remember that?'

'Was long time ago an yu never once wrote me. How me to know whether yu dead or 'live? Yu not sorry? How yu could leave your pickney, dem? Your girl chile a likkle, likkle baby? Yu got more?' There was bitter accusation in his tone.

'That's why I never came back, Robert. Never wrote to you. I did miss them, especially Sharon. If I had come back, I could not have left again.'

'You planned behind my back.'

'How could I tell you? You would not have let me go.'

'I give yu everyting you wanted. An I woulda let yu go iffn yu asked me. Yu was dere mother. How yu could leave dem like yu did?'

'I am still their mother.'

'No.'

He sat up, his eyes ablaze now, more alive than he had been for many months.

'Dey mine. I brung dem up. I did it widdout yu. Yu forget three bwoys yu had an one baby girl. An yu lef me to do everyting. I coulda let de social take them. But me didn't. Don't yu ever say dey yours.'

'I carried them for nine months, suffered the birth pains, fed them.'

'No. Yu lef dem wid me. I had more pain dan yu will ever know every day an night after yu gone till dey grown people.' Before she could speak again he told her to go. 'Jus leave me alone let me tink.'

Once again he watched the upright straight back walk away from him. She was so proud.

'Wait.' He reached for the photograph that sat on the bedside locker. He held it towards her.

'See dem? Tek it, tek it.'

He was sure that there were tears in her eyes when she stretched out her hand and took the metal-framed picture. It was a family photograph taken three years previously when Devon had visited them. Robert sat surrounded by his children and grandchildren. Sharon on one side her arm resting comfortably along the back of the studio chair, young Rebecca in his lap and the rest of the family either kneeling or sitting close by. Sharon suggested the photograph be taken.

'Because we don't often have the pleasure of big brother spending time in this country with us and we haven't got a complete family photograph.'

The irony of those words came back to him now. He recalled the conversation between his daughter and himself shortly before his accident.

'All these years and the girl never aks about she mudder.'
His thoughts were interrupted by a gasp.

'You mean I have grandchildren?'

'You don't have nuttin.'

'Oh my lord, look at them. Just look at them. Robert.'

'Tek de picture an go. When yu come in here, yu is jus de ward sister, nuttin else.'

'I am still your wife, Robert. We are still married, aren't we?'

Closing his eyes, he listened for the swish and soft thud of the door before allowing himself to exhale. There had never seemed time to go and look about getting a divorce.

22

January and February, crisp frosty days followed by rain and wind eventually gave way to a blustery March that reminded Doris of her childhood. She spent a of lot time engrossed in her thoughts these days. Perhaps, she argued, that's what growing old is all about. Thinking about the past while trying not to think of the future. I am sixty two years old. What future is there for me? I don't feel my age, but how do I know what I should feel? I have never been this age before. My children treat me as if I am in my dotage while I want to act like a lovesick teenager. It is five months since I last saw Robert and every day I wake with him on my mind. Thoughts of him are with me most of the day and I dream about him at night. Surely someone my age is not supposed to have such feelings.

When I listen to Amy's many passing innuendoes, and when I join in with her comments about the men at the club, I have my doubts. Amy implies that with a man friend she would still, you know, do it. I haven't done it for such a long time I don't know if I could. Who would want to with an old woman like me? There you go, Doris, referring to yourself as old again. I wonder if Robert regards me as old. If we were a couple, would we? Could we? Would I? Should I? I wonder what it would be like doing it after all these years. Would it be different doing it with him instead of with another man, with Frank if he were still alive or with Robert who is black? Stop this nonsense, Doris, you should not be thinking thoughts like this at your age. There I go again putting my age before my feelings.

She rinsed her cup and plate, carefully dried them and placed them in the cupboard. She hung the teatowel on the rack. Was he a creature of habit like her? Did men develop routines and habits as they aged?

She remembered Frank and the things he insisted on her doing. She was suddenly struck by the influence he had been on what she did during the first years of her marriage. Even ways she learned from her mother as good housekeeping, changed into being done the way his mother did them. Instead of folding down the collars of his shirts and ironing them flat, she ironed them and left them standing upright for him to fold down when he put one on. His socks were folded, not tucked one inside the other. He always complained if she poured milk into his cup before the tea and he liked his cup rinsed with warm water first. Kept the tea warmer, longer, he claimed.

Doris smiled to herself, recalling telling Robert of this idiosyncrasy. He, in turn, told her of his own father and how as a boy it was his responsibility to carry an enamel mug full of hot coffee to him every morning wherever he was on his land admiring the growing provisions. His father always berated him because by the time he found him, the coffee was always cold. One morning determined to get it right, Robert put the mug briefly into the oven. After filling it with scalding coffee he wrapped a small towel around the mug and carefully carried it to his father who was examining the stalks of sugar cane at the far end of the lot.

'Good morning, daddy. Yu coffee heah.' Placing the mug on an upturned bucket he turned and ran towards the house calling over his shoulder that he had left the coffee. By the time his father reached home, calling urgently to his wife for some 'vaseline' for his 'skinned lip', Robert was on his way to school. His daddy never ever complained again. Neither did he mention his peeling lip. Robert, however, was keenly aware that his father did not begin his day with an orange newly picked from his own tree for several days.

Pulling on her coat, Doris realized that most men were the cause of changes in women when they married them but men seldom if ever changed their pre-marriage habits, rituals or lifestyles.

As she walked towards the bus stop, she was seized with a feeling of renewal. Perhaps it was the clear blue sky from which the sun shone amazingly warm for a March day. Or it might have been the rows of nodding daffodils edging the dog patch. Everywhere was newly green interspersed with white or pink blossom that fluttered to the ground like snowflakes each time the wind blew. There was a sense of purpose in her step as she neared the zebra crossing. She heard herself humming 'Que Sera, Sera' when she hailed the bus. She smiled at the driver as she showed him her pass. 'Lovely day!' She paused, waiting for a reply; forcing a response from the blank eyes. 'Makes you feel glad to be alive, a day like this doesn't it? A day of new beginnings.'

His gloved hand pulled on the hand brake. The other one turned the wheel, the bus roared into life. All in a matter of seconds. Yet it had taken time before the driver acknowledged her greeting. 'What? Oh yes, 'bout time we saw the sun.' Eyes already turned towards the road. Doris staggered, almost fell onto the long seat as the bus lurched forward up the hill heading for Crystal Palace.

The previous week she had finally found a way to try and contact Robert. It was so simple she was amazed at the fact she hadn't thought of it before. Just contact the different clubs for pensioners in Lewisham. There couldn't be that many whose patrons were from the Caribbean. And then it would be all plain sailing. Knowing which area of the borough he lived and remembering what he told her about his journey simplified matters.

'A bus to Catford then a short walk up George Lane,' the female voice on the other end of the line directed her. 'You can't miss the building. It's on the right side of the road, just past 'The George' public house. Looks fairly new amongst the houses along there.'

'Thank you, thank you.'

Remembering how her heart fluttered and her voice was all breathy made her blush.

'No problem. You're welcome. See you soon,' the faceless voice came over the line.

'I wonder if she thought I was a prospective client?'

Standing in front of the entrance, Doris pulled at her coat, smoothed it down and then patted her hair, a pattern of movement that was as familiar to Robert as it was unconscious to her. She took a deep breath. The reception desk was empty. The door beyond it stood ajar. Female voices came from inside. A shriek, followed by a giggle and then raucous laughter. Doris noticed a hand attached to a bangle-encircled wrist. Ringed fingers clutched the door frame. Was there an arm and a body that belonged to the hand? You can buy replicas of fingers to fasten to car boots. Perhaps this was a trick one fixed to door jambs so that people would believe they were going to be attended to soon, that they were not alone. She felt suddenly alone looking at the brown hand clutching the white metal frame. It struck home that this was a club for pensioners of African or Caribbean origin. She was neither. They might not let her in.

To her right, through the open double doors, she heard murmuring voices, music and a sharp slapping sound accompanied by men's loud voices. There was a vaguely familiar smell. Food. How long since she smelt Robert's aftershave? The food he brought for her to taste on picnics?

Uncertain, she stood waiting. Panicked, she clutched her bag with both hands and looked for a bell. She cleared her throat, waited ten seconds, cleared her throat again.

'Excuse me, hello.' Laughter again. Could they see her? Were they laughing at her?

'Hello.'

Doris jumped, gasped and leant forward. She put her hand on the counter to steady herself.

'She too busy to hear you, love. What you want?' The voice was behind her.

'Oh.' She turned quickly and almost lost her balance again when the familiar Jamaican accent hit her ears. It wasn't him. Couldn't possibly have been him. Taller, wider, a different smile, different hands. How long since she held his hand?

'I was looking for, making enquiries about, a friend of mine who comes here. I ...'

'Jus go in, love. Don't wait on them. You'll be there for ever if you do. Who you want to see?'

'His name is Rob...'

'Can I help you?' The owner of the hand stood across from her. The hand now rested on the wooden counter. Doris's eyes travelled up the arm to the shoulder draped in a piece of yellow and green Kente, to the gold hooped earrings and finally to the mouth and eyes framed by a myriad of fine braids.

'She says she looking for somebody.' The tall man behind her answered the receptionist while she searched for her tongue.

'Somebody here?'
She nodded.

'You know this club is for people who come from...'

Yes, I know that.' Then sharply, 'Does that mean I can't come in whether I want to join or not?'

'Why you want to join?' Tall man, no longer behind her was leaning against the counter.

'Mind you business, man, and let the lady talk.' Turning to her again, the receptionist chupped. 'Yes, what can I do for you, lady?'

'I'm trying to, I'm looking for a friend of mine. He said he came to a club for black pensioners. I'm not sure if this is the right place but I don't think he would travel to the Moonshot or Telegraph Hill.'

'Is a man you looking for, lady?' Tall man again. His smile showed a gold tooth set in perfectly even teeth. 'If you can't find him, I'm free and willing.'

'George, go away and leave the lady in peace or I'll tell Mrs George how you've taken to flirting with little white ladies in your spare time instead of doing your work about the place.'

They both laughed as he bent to pick up a plastic crate containing cleaning materials before walking across the lobby and disappearing through a small door marked 'Caretaker'.

Doris began again trying to make her request sound perfectly reasonable as opposed to a love quest. Calling to someone in the inner room, the receptionist introduced her to the club secretary who, after consulting her records confirmed that there was a Robert Williams on the club membership but that he hadn't been for a while.

'Not since before Christmas. He wasn't at the party. His gift was one of the ones we put in the store room. We really only keep a check on those who get brought in by bus. He didn't used to come on the blue buses, did he?'

Doris shook her head. Things were not looking as hopeful now.

'Come.' The secretary lifted the counter and took her arm. 'Let's go and ask inside. Someone must know about him.'

Every table in the large, light, airy room was occupied. Lunch was over and the tables which were of differing sizes were being cleared. Her eyes swept the room. She had never seen so many older black people together before. In fact until that precise moment Doris would have confessed to being unaware of any pensioners of colour except for Robert. Young people, yes. Middle aged, yes. But old black people, the thought had never occurred to her. Now before her eyes were people of her age and older, some much older. Several were in wheelchairs. Some looked as if they had been the victims of a stroke. There were white sticks visible. So were walking frames and tripods.

From a large table set in the sunny bay window, a roar erupted followed by a crash as dominoes bounced upwards before falling back onto the table top. Doris turned. No women sat there. Just as Robert had told her, the men's backs formed a barrier to the rest of the room. Anxiously her eyes roamed the room. She knew already he wouldn't be there. Now she looked for someone of the same skin colour as her. They all looked at her. Eyes followed her. From faces of almost ebony black through to mahogany red and creamy white. Hats and caps of every description. Hairstyles ranging from intricately braided designs to simple natural haircuts. Grey locks, grey curls, black braids, smooth wigs, carefully combed to carefully wrapped. No familiar faces here.

Except for the men playing dominoes who were oblivious to the rest of the room, everywhere was suddenly quiet. Embroidery needles were held poised to make the next stitch, crochet hooks ceased to flash, knitting needles were stilled. The dealing of playing cards halted and newspapers were laid down upon the formica surfaces.

The secretary left her and went to the domino players. How long was she there talking to the only people who showed no interest in her intrusion? Laughter rose from the men. Doris watched as the woman leaned down and put her arm around the shoulders of one of the men. She patted the back of another and playfully slapped away the hand of the man in a wheelchair when he attempted to pat her behind.

She crossed the room again, this time stopping to speak with several women. All the women looked in her direction. No-one smiled at her. Heads nodded, lips moved, necks bent forward to confer. One of the women pointed at another table. Doris turned again as the secretary strolled to the table indicated.

She waited. A woman was talking now. A tiny woman with fine features, wearing glasses perched at the end of her nose. When she spoke her head nodded vigorously rather like a bird. The navy blue hat trimmed with lace bobbed up and down. Already people were losing interest in Doris who stood conspicuously alone, feeling very white and very vulnerable, wondering if she had done the right thing.

They were beckoning to her to come to the table. The secretary brought a chair, asked if she would like a cup of tea or anything, introduced her to Miss Pinkney who might be able to help. None of the ladies asked her why she was looking for Robert. They all introduced themselves, offering a hand to shake while watching her closely with knowing eyes.

Miss Pinkney said,

'Last time I saw him was Christmas evening. Him did come to the church with him fambily. All o dem, even the little pickney. Was nice to see how dem a grow. Him done a good good job bringin up his fambily dem widdout no mudder. He looked good too, ceptin him could hardly walk. His two big sons almost carry him down to the seat.' She shook her head sympathetically. The others nodded in agreement.

Doris wondered what she should say or do. Ask a question or wait until more information was offered.

'Him have a hoperation on his leg after he fall down and break a bone. Is me cousin Priscilla tell me, she been visitin him in the hospital.'

Doris was aware of her hand gripping the table. The voices faded away.

That last time, after the dance, the tea dance. Robert leaning heavily on his stick as he struggled homeward in the rain swam before her eyes.

'O dear.'

'Him still in the hospital, you know.'

'No, I didn't know. The last time I saw him was in November. We lost touch.' She waited not knowing how to continue.

Miss Pinkney was fumbling in her handbag. She withdrew a small diary and began to flick over the pages.

'You got some paper?'

Doris opened her own bag. She searched in vain for a piece of paper, remembering that other scrap of paper on which a telephone number had been written. Finally taking out her pension book she turned it over and handed it to the woman.

'This Miss Priscilla's number. Tell her is me give you the number and she will tell you what hospital him in.'

Her disappointment at not finding Robert at the club was tempered by the knowledge that she would soon establish where he was and be able to visit him. First thing when she got home, she would ring the telephone number and speak to this Priscilla. Who was Priscilla anyway? Was she the real reason Robert hadn't contacted her? No matter, her heart was singing, she was getting closer.

23

Sitting dozing beside his bed Robert was startled awake by someone touching him. Confused for a moment, he thought he was at home in his own chair. It took a few seconds for him to get his bearings and to realize that Nadia was standing in front of him. He knew immediately that she was not in the room on matters relating to his health or welfare. Since the day he had given her the photograph they had maintained a strictly professional relationship.

All his treatment was carried out by other nurses. She never entered his room unaccompanied and he totally ignored her when he left the room and shuffled slowly past the office to the day room. When the other nurses sung out 'Morning Mr Williams' or 'How you doing Robert?' he responded accordingly. He addressed them directly by name. And he never added her name or title or spoke directly to her. If the ward staff noticed, no remark was passed within her hearing. She was senior management, therefore gossiping about her in public was more than any one dared to do.

'Can I sit down, Robert?'

'What yu want?'

'I wanted to ask you if you have told them, the children, who I am?'

'Should I have?'

'No, no it's just that when they come to visit, I...'

'You what?'

'I want to speak to them, to say hello, ask them about themselves, you know.'

'No, I don't know. You never wanted to speak to them before or ask them what they doing. Why now? Sposing me never come in dis blasted hospital. Sposing me did get better without any problems an me discharged before you come back from your holiday? We woulda never seen each other and life woulda go on eh.'

'But it hasn't happened like that, Robert. Perhaps we were meant to meet again and have another chance.'

'What you mean 'another chance'? Aint no chances where you an me is concerned. Was finished long time. Was you left me, remember? Jus cos me never divorce you...'

'I didn't mean you and me having another chance. I can understand that. However, our children are adults now and surely they have a right to meet and know their mother.'

'You don't have no rights as their mother.'

'Please Robert try and understand.'

'Is only one thing me understand and that is yu lef yu children when dem was likkle babies and you never once come back or write.'

'Listen, perhaps it wouldn't have been so bad if there weren't any grandchildren. But I see them going by and I want to speak to them.'

'Well, wont be a problem after tomorrow, will it? Cos the doctor tell me I can discharge tomorrow. So you can sit in your office and not be distracted. Anyway, you tellin me you neva have anoda man an no more pickney?'

'I left you, Robert, because I wanted a career. The babies came too soon. Listen. I am being honest with you. I truly believe that some force has meant us to cross paths again. If not for you and me to be reconciled, then for your, our children.'

'No.'

'Robert they are adults. You have to tell them. Let them make up their own minds. They have a right.'

'First, they never aks about you.'

'That doesn't mean they don't want to know. Let me know my own grandchildren, please I beg you.'

'Second, you never tink about their rights before.'

She made no effort to wipe away the tears that were beginning to flow down her cheeks.

'Robert, please. What do you want me to do? Say I'm sorry?'

'Yu already told me. Yu not sorry.'

'You know that's not what I meant.'

'Is there diffrent types of sorry den?'

She wiped her cheeks with the back of her hand.

'Alright. Yes, I am sorry I left you to bring up the children alone. I am sorry that I missed them growing up, missed them marrying, missed their whole lives.' She leant across to his locker and took a tissue from the box. 'But I am not sorry that I fulfilled my ambition, Robert Williams, and I want the chance to explain, to tell my children. Surely you can't deny me that.'

'Leave me alone.'

'Can I keep the photograph, Robert?'

'Go away.' Turning his head, he refused to acknowledge her tears.

Alone in his room, Robert pulled himself upright from the chair and grabbed for his stick. He shook his head and clenched his fist. Fuelled by anger, he began to limp furiously along the ward and found himself progressing at a speed that he hadn't achieved for several years.

'Take care, Mr Williams,' a nurse called out. 'We don't want you falling over now, do we?'

Robert didn't hear her. Neither did he hear the outer door of the ward when it slammed back against the wall as he pushed through it narrowly missing an incoming visitor. He jabbed fiercely at the lift button again and again. He was determined to get away from her. As far away as possible. He would make his way outside into the open air.

'Come on, come on!' Robert jabbed again at the unblinking eye on the wall. A bell rang and a few seconds later the doors of the lift slid open. Head down like an angry bull, he charged forward.

'Robert!'

The familiar voice jerked his head upwards. Standing partly in and out of the lift, they gazed at each other. Doris recovered herself as the doors began to slide shut. She pressed the hold button.

'Oh, my dear!' She held him then, her face buried deep in the front of his paisley night shirt. Robert encircled her with his arms as he braced himself to stay upright. He was speechless. Doris felt his heart pounding against her chest. Her own matched the rhythm.

Hand in hand they returned to the ward oblivious of eyes that turned and watched them walking slowly towards his room. Doris sat on his bed in the same place his previous visitor had sat.

'How did you find me?' At last he could speak.

Doris told him of the telephone calls, the visit to the club, the conversation with Sister Priscilla.

'Who yu, den?'

'I'm a friend of R...Mr Williams.'

'Who yu say give yu mi number?'

'A Miss Pinkney at the Calabash club.'

'Is what yu want to contact mi friend for.'

Doris detected the emphasis on *friend*.

'He been ill in the hospital for a long time. Is how come yu never look for him before?'

'I have been trying for months. Please.'

'Me should aks him permission first before me tell yu what hospital him is in.'

'Look dear,' Doris tried to keep her voice from rising, 'if you wont tell me which hospital he is in, I can always ring round to find out for myself.'

It was so obvious that she couldn't imagine why she hadn't thought of it before. She would not have needed to worry about speaking to Priscilla. Because to be truthful she had been apprehensive about speaking to her, particularly as she didn't know if the preceding months of silence were because Robert and Priscilla were together. Priscilla's persistence might have paid off after all.

'And on my way up here, I bumped into my son-in-law,' she now told him. 'I was waiting for the lift. Fancy having an orthopedic ward on the top floor of a hospital. I heard this voice call to me and coming down the corridor was my daughter Joan's husband.' Doris had prayed the lift would open before he could reach her. But no such luck. She was surprised to see him because she hadn't been aware that anyone in the family was attending the hospital. He told her that Billy had been in a lot of pain recently. The family doctor thought that there could be some sort of problem with scar tissue from when he had his appendix out. 'Remember that weekend when I should have come to dinner at your house? A year or so ago. Anyway, Billy needed an appointment with a consultant and they decided it was quicker to come up and make the appointment in person.' When Alan wanted to know what she was doing, she told him that she was going to see an old friend. No-one he knew, though. But he had the afternoon free so he said that if she met him at the entrance in an hour he would run her home. 'That's nice of him, isn't it? Look, Robert, yesterday I went to Brixton market, I brought this especially for you.' Doris had remembered what Robert told her about the smell of a mango and how to hold one in her hand to see if it was ripe. Reaching down she lifted up and opened a plastic carrier bag from which she produced a large rosy mango.

'This is just for you.' Robert looked at her and smiled.

He recounted all that had befallen him during the previous six months. He told her how he had racked his brains trying to think of a way to contact her. He pulled a small note book from his bedside locker and tore a page from it. The he wrote his address and telephone number on it. Now you have both. I am going home tomorrow, so you will be able to keep in touch.'

'I promise.'

Robert stood, 'Let me walk with you to the door.'

'Should you?'

'Yes, they tell me I must keep mobile an you know what they been doin with me?'

Before she could respond, he told her. 'Takin me in the hospital swimmin pool.'

'So we will be able to go again. Oh, I have missed my Wednesdays, Robert.'

Outside the office, Robert paused. He looked at the straight back, as slim as it was the first day he set eyes on it.

'Hold on. Sister? Hexscuse me, Sister.'

She swung round on the swivel chair. There was no trace of the earlier tears. On the ledge above the desk he saw the photograph. It hadn't been there the previous evening.

'I will tell the children when they come tonight and they can make their own decision.'

With his free hand, he took Doris's own and slowly began to make his way down the ward. There would be plenty of time to explain to Doris.

Standing waiting for the lift, she knew for certain the meaning of only being as old as you feel. Right there and then she felt about seventeen and it was a glorious feeling. The lift doors opened.

See you next Wednesday, dear.' Leaning forward she placed a kiss on his lips.

'Mother!'

The horror and shock in her son-in-law's voice was unmistakable. As she stepped into the lift, Doris blew a defiant kiss at Robert and turned to face her stunned relative.

24

The journey home was made in silence. Feigning a terrible headache, Doris asked her son-in-law, Alan, to take her straight home. She asked him to give her love to Billy and promised to see him at the weekend. In a state of shock, Alan had not been able to find a way to make conversation with her. He had waited for almost twenty minutes past the hour he had given her. And only then decided to make his way up the ward having told himself that she did not have to leave with him. After all, she had obviously made her own way to the hospital. He really couldn't understand why Joan and the others made such fuss about the old girl. She seemed quite able to look after herself. Yet they made her out to be more or less helpless. As far as he could see, there was nothing helpless about the way she had planted that kiss on that black man's lips. But what would the girls say when he told them and really he didn't know how he was going to tell them. They would have forty fits just to know that there was a man friend. As for his colour!

'Sly old bag, I wonder how long this has been going on,' he snorted.

Doris knew that there would be a confrontation and it would come sooner or later. Nothing was said when Joan telephoned to arrange who would pick her up for the drive out to Westerham where the family was to celebrate her son-in-law's birthday with lunch together in a Carvery. Perhaps he hasn't told her yet. I know my daughter. She couldn't keep it to herself a minute longer than necessary. Likes to think she is in charge. I wonder where she gets it from. Certainly not me. Must have inherited it from her father. Keeping her finger on the button and controlling everyone in the family.

Without any reference to the hospital, Joan answered Doris's questions regarding Billy's state of health. Was she avoiding mentioning it?

'They have given him something for the pain. He'll probably go in for an exploratory operation in the next few weeks. The doctors seem pretty certain that it is just a bit of scar tissue from the appendectomy he had. Remember?'

She could hardly have forgotten. The Sunday meal that never transpired because of the emergency.

'All in all young Billy, though you may not realize it, you have played quite a part in my love life,' she said, putting down the telephone. And then Doris was overcome by a fit of the giggles. 'My love life! Listen to me! Hysterical. What on earth am I worried about? I am older than them and I am worried about what they will do when they find out.'

Wiping away tears of mirth, she asked herself the question she'd asked herself many times during the past few months. What was she going to say to them? More importantly, she wondered what she was going to do. Perhaps stick up for herself at last.

Sunday passed. A pleasant few hours, a gentle stroll around the village talking about everything and nothing before driving home where there was more food and a cake. Doris had baked and decorated it herself. Throughout the day, Doris waited for Joan to drop the bombshell. She watched and listened to her children. She searched for clues that would tell her that they knew her secret. Still she remained unsure whether there was an undercurrent of tension or not.

Once or twice she caught her son-in-law looking at her. Unable to read his face, she averted her eyes. She waited for the inevitable storm to break knowing that she was not going to bring up the subject herself. Finally Doris decided that perhaps he had not found the nerve to tell her daughter.

'Mum,'

They were seated around the dining table waiting for the kettle to boil. Aha! Making sure she has everyone's attention. And there is no escape for me, either, because Billy has been delegated to make tea.

'Yes, dear.'

Doris brushed away an imaginary crumb. But the table had to be clean. Doris herself had shaken the cloth after breakfast.

'I didn't know you knew anyone in hospital.'

Pause.

'Alan said that when he went to make the appointment for Billy he bumped into you at the hospital.'

'That's right.'

Pause.

'It's not anyone we know?'

'No.'

Doris hovered between waiting to let her daughter actually say the words and making it easier for her.

'Is it some visiting scheme you belong to?'

'No.'

'Well.'

'What did Alan tell you?'

The silence was broken only by the sound of the clock on the mantelpiece.

'I think you know what he told me, mum.'

'Does everyone else know what it is that Joan is finding so difficult to put into words?'

Her eyes travelled around the table. None of her children would look at her.

'Mum.'

'Who's going to start then, you or Alan? I can't believe that you have all managed to suppress your curiosity for the whole day. Ah, that's it. You didn't want to spoil Alan's day, did you?'

She heard the defiance in her voice and grew determined to stay on top; to take charge.'

'But we know, mum,' Anne spoke.

Doris placed both her hands firmly on the table as if to brace herself. 'Know what?'

'Oh come on, mum. Tell them.'

'What do you want me tell you? Alan saw me visiting a friend at the hospital. Is there anything wrong with that?'

'He seemed like a very good friend according to Alan.'

'He is.'

'You kissed him.'

'And?'

'Well it's just that, mum, Alan said that it was a coloured man.'

'That's right.'

'We didn't know you had any coloured friends.'

'Is there nothing in my life that is private? Am I supposed to tell you everything?'

'You were holding his hand, mum.'

'Pity you didn't come right on to the ward you would have seen more.'

'Mother!'

'You are the person implying that I have done something wrong, Joan.'

'No I wasn't, mum, it's just that you haven't told us about this friend person and from what Alan said you appeared to be very good friends.'

'He's right.'

'Mum, will you stop being defensive and tell us what's going on.' Peter gently placed his hand on her arm.

'What do you want to know?'

'Well, if we put two and two together we can assume that you have known this man for a while. How long and when? Oh I don't know. Just tell us, mum.'

'He is the person I was going out with every week until he fell ill.'

'We all thought you were going out with one of your friends from the lunch club.'

'Does he go to your club?'

'No.'

'Then where did you meet him, mum?'

'Actually I met him one day at the Paxton roundabout on the way up to the Palace.'

'You mean he picked you up?' John, her youngest son spoke for the first time, winking at her.

Doris noticed that he was going bald in the same place as his dad. It is funny, she thought, just how much he had grown to look like him. Same hint of a paunch, too, creeping over the waistband of his jeans. Mind you, his father would never have worn jeans.

'If you like, yes. He picked me up.'

Her daughter and daughter-in-law looked aghast.

'And he's a Jamaican,' she added for good measure. Did the silence last ten seconds or ten minutes?

'So he is black?' Which of her children finally managed to speak?

'Most Jamaicans are. We have been going out together for almost two years. We enjoy each other's company. I like him very much and I plan to carry on seeing him.'

There! It was said. Finally out it had come out. Tumbled in a rush of words out of her mouth, filling the air surrounding her and them, echoing, resounding from smooth tablecloth to white ceiling and back again. Her words had smacked each of them in the face. She even wanted to add, a 'So there.' But Doris managed to restrain herself and looked, instead, at each in turn: Joan ashen faced, Alan staring at the place mat in front of him. Anne gazing at her with eyes ready to pop. And a scarlet-faced Peter struggled to keep his jaw from dropping. How convenient that the grandchildren were all in the kitchen helping Billy.

'Mum, you sound just like a rebellious teenager.' Her eldest son finally found his voice.

'Probably no different to you when your father or I forbade you to do something,' was her retort.

'I always thought that it was a woman friend you were going out with each week. Another widow.' Anne tried to keep her voice from rising.

'Well now you know that it is a man friend, don't you?'

'That's not it, mum.'

'Of course I know that's not what it is that is bothering you.'

'How could you, mum?' Anne's voice was becoming shrill. Her husband, Martin, put his hand on her arm. He was embarrassed by the whole thing really. After all, she was getting on a bit but what she did was her business and there was no way he would talk to his mother like that and carry on the way her family were. Not that his mother would have a black man as a friend. Come to think of it, never in his wildest fantasies could he have ever imagined Doris getting close enough to a black man to kiss him. He didn't know whose side he should take. So he kept his hand on Anne's arm and his mouth shut.

'Dad must be turning in his grave.' Peter joined the chorus of protests that seemed to be rising up like a wall in front of Doris.

'He can't do that if he was cremated.'

Billy, who having heard the raised voices, had left his sister and cousins in the kitchen and crept back into the dining room, carefully positioning himself down on the floor close to the fireplace hoping not to be seen, gave himself away.

'This, young man is nothing to do with you.' His father rounded on him and ordered him from the room. As he was about to leave, Billy turned and asked his grandmother,

'Does he like Reggae music, Nan?'

Doris felt a wave of laughter rise which she tried to suppress.

'Mum this is no laughing matter.'

Joan tried to regain control by modulating her voice. Doris was reminded of Margaret Thatcher.

'What I do with my time should not affect either the living or the dead.'

She spoke calmly and quietly.

Joan opened her mouth to remonstrate with her mother again. But it was John who spoke.

'We care about you, mum. Surely we should be concerned about who you go out with and who you invite into your home. After all, you only have to read the papers to see the consequences.'

'I didn't say I had brought anyone here and if I had why should you be concerned about me bringing a sixty-odd year old man into my home? I am not child. I am your mother. I have managed to bring you all up and cope on my own for the past ten years.'

'Mother,' Peter was trying to keep himself from shouting. 'You said that this man picked you up. How can you know that he is not a confidence trickster or that he doesn't have a family? Everybody knows what crooks most of the young black men are. You only have to look at the press and the television. Have you thought about the possibility of drugs?'

Doris, about to acknowledge that, yes, some of these thoughts had surfaced, was silenced by her grandson's outraged voice.

'Is that what you think about my friends, dad and Uncle Peter? How come you have never stopped Alex and Tyrone from coming in? I bet Maxie Browne wouldn't want to buy you a drink at the club if he could hear you talking about black people now.'

'That's not the same. Anyway, I thought I told you to go to the other room.'

'Billy, you have already been told. This has nothing to do with you.' John and Joan spoke in unison.

Billy stood his ground. 'Nan, they think he is going to con you into giving him your house.' He rounded on his parents, his uncle and aunts. 'It's really because he is black, isn't it, dad, mum?'

'Billy go into the kitchen and make the tea. There's a love,' Doris spoke wearily. What was happening here? Had she really raised such a selfish bunch of children? She couldn't believe what she was hearing. Clearly, the colour of her friend was the only issue. They all had their own homes and families. All had been treated fairly by her and their father. They'd been encouraged to study, work hard at school, join in community activities, treat people as they found them and most of all, respect their elders.

She was independent. She owed them nothing. She asked them for nothing. They were the ones who telephoned and suggested that they would come round on Sunday, that they would all go out for a drive if the weather was good the following weekend. That perhaps she would like to go away for a few days with them. They had already booked her a room, well, a bed really, as she would have to share with Jason and Paula. 'It's cheaper that way, mum,' which meant that they wouldn't have to use the hotel sitter service. Or would it be all right if Simon spent Friday night with her? 'We have an offer of a night out with the firm and he doesn't want to stay at his other Nans.'

Billy's question hung unanswered, hovering in the twilight. He went into the kitchen but made sure that the door was left slightly ajar.

'I suppose I could attach myself to a person with a disability of any sort. You would all tolerate me being friends with an ex-con or something, even a foreigner just so long as the person is not black. Am I right?'

'Mum!'

Whatever Joan was about to say was interrupted by the kitchen door opening. Billy entered carrying a tray bearing the birthday cake, forty candles blazing. Jason, Paula and Simon followed singing 'Happy birthday to you.'

At last the house was quiet. Closing the front door, Doris returned to her sitting room and sank onto the settee. She shut her eyes and tried to order her thoughts and make some sense of the day. Silence truly was golden. And the rest of the world cared not one jot about another widow in her sixties. Her children were really more concerned about what other people might say, how such a relationship might affect her grandchildren; and whether her friends knew. Doris thought of her grandchildren who attended schools with children whose origins were from all over the world. Billy's closest friend was black. The two boys came together on Saturday mornings to chat and run errands. The family did not object to that friendship. So their reaction to her disclosure meant something else. She was still not sure where she had found the strength from to counter their arguments. Now that they had finally left, she felt absolutely drained.

They had consumed tea and cake while the atmosphere crackled with unspoken thoughts. Each of her children gave their official reasons for objecting to Doris's friendship. But they had to finally admit that they did not mind her having a male friend, 'If that's what you want or need mother. Though until now, we always thought you were contented. I am speaking for all of us, am I not?'

Joan raised her eyebrows knowingly while sweeping the faces of the adults seated at the table.

'I am sure the others will agree with me if I come out and say that I cannot condone you having a black person as close as you are implying. I think you understand what I am trying to say, mum.'

'So, it seems I have to seek your permission to have a sexual relationship.'

She could hear the sound of the television in the next room where Billy, even though he was desperate to listen to the adults, had taken charge of his cousins. Joan gasped. Her face turned scarlet. She opened and closed her mouth like a fish out of water. For once she was speechless. The only time her mother had talked about sex to her was when she was in her early teens experiencing her first periods. Then Doris had told her how babies were made and why women menstruated. Now her mother was actually bringing up the subject in front of Alan and the others. Her face burned with embarrassment. She wished the encounter in the hospital had never happened.

'Mum, it has got nothing to do with sex. If you want to sleep with someone you ... though I thought you were'

'Past it?'

'No. I'

'Look, Joan'

Alan tried to interrupt, 'God, I wish I never told you now.'

'I can well believe that. Imagine if it was your own mother having an affair.'

'Hold on. No-one said that mum was having an affair.' Peter appealed to his sisters.

'I am not saying you can't. You can have as many friends as you want, mum.'

'Just as long as they are not men, full stop. Or black men.'

'I think we should be going home before someone says something they will regret.' Martin stood up.

'Can we just clear this up and confirm what we feel and where we stand on this issue?'

John looked at his Mother.

'I think it is important to clarify the situation.'

'Would you like me to leave the room while you take a vote?' Her voice seem to come from a long way off.

'There is no need for you to get upset, mum.'

'We just want you to consider our feelings and point of view. As a family we are not happy with you having a relationship with this man. If you want a male friend that is okay with us but we want you to end this friendship and stop making a spectacle of yourself in public. Imagine the embarrassment if someone who knows us sees you out holding his hand or something. We are your family and you should put us first.' Joan looked at the others for support.

'Sounds to me as if you came to this decision before today. Now, I think it would be best for all of us if you left me alone.'

Standing woodenly on the doorstep receiving their farewell kisses, Doris remained mute.

'Think about it please, mum,' said Anne as her lips brushed across her mother's cheek.

'It's for the best, really,' Joan murmured trying to hug the stiff body.

'I'm sorry,' was all Alan could utter when he backed off the step and down the path.

'And now here I am.' Doris stood resolutely, straightened her dress, patted her hair and went into the hallway where she put on her jacket. She glanced at the clock but the time did not register.

It took her two hours that Sunday evening to make a journey to Brockley that normally took, at most, twenty five minutes. While she stood on the parade recalling the first meeting, a young woman holding a squirming toddler commented about the infrequency of the buses. 'Must be only two running today and we've missed both of 'em,' she grumbled jiggling the fretful youngster up and down. Doris checked her handbag for the address. Yes, it was safe in the little note book she had taken to carrying with her.

Robert prepared for bed in sombre mood. He felt extraordinarily tired. Not because this was his first weekend at home after many months but because the children and their mother had come together for a reunion in the family home.

His resistance had been worn down by Sharon who said it was the only place they could meet to fight the demons of accusations and recrimination before any healing could take place. He was not so sure he wanted there to be any healing.

'I kept my word, told you about her and where she was. I don't want to tek up where she left off. She cause me plenty, plenty hurt.'

'We know that, dad, and we appreciate your feelings. A neutral place like a restaurant won't give us the time we need and we are not ready either to take her to our own homes. This is where she left us, daddy. Let her face us here.'

Sharon's emotions were in a turmoil regarding the mother she could not remember. She stroked his hand. The shock she experienced when Robert introduced Nadia that evening when she went to the hospital with his clothes in readiness for the following day had been indescribable. There was nothing that could have prepared her. And the coincidence! Well.

'I was stunned, Devon,' she later told her brother when she called him in New York. None of them were able to talk coherently on the ward. So the decision was reached, after much persuasion, for a meeting the following Sunday in Robert's home.

Sharon prepared dinner. She insisted that Robert was still convalescent. They and their children assembled and waited for Nadia to arrive. There were no warm hugs from her children though Nadia was able to kiss her grandchildren. Conversation at first was stilted, and limited to talk about children, and schooling. It was only after dinner when everyone was sitting with coffee that Sharon in her usual forthright manner asked Nadia why she left them. An electrifying hush descended. Robert, clearing his throat in his customary way, shifted his position to accommodate his still stiff leg. It seemed as if everyone in the room, apart from him, had ceased to breathe. Once again he heard Nadia's reasons for leaving her children, her home and him. For her children, it was the first time they had an explanation for the wall erected by their father.

They listened. And when at last Nadia ceased speaking, there was a moment when no-one was able to speak.

Sharon said, 'I always thought you were dead.'

'Didn't you tell her about me?'

'What could me say bout you? There was nuttin to tell.'

'We didn't like to talk about you to dad,' Steven added.

'Did you get what it was that you wanted?' Aston could not bring himself to call her mother.

'Well you can see I have a senior position. I've done a lot more in between.'

'You didn't have to leave us to achieve that.' The anger in Steven's voice crackled like burning timber.

'I know that I could not have been a mother to you and studied for a career.

'Other people do. Have done. And daddy ended up being mother, father and provider.' Sharon echoed her father's thoughts. He sat stony faced. There was nothing for him to say. Nothing Nadia could say to justify leaving him.

'What do you want me to say? I can ask you to forgive me for leaving you all when you were only babies. I knew what I wanted. That was why I came to England. Making babies wasn't in my plans.'

'Then why did you have us? Why didn't you stop at one?'

'You make it sound so easy. I can see you are all angry at me for leaving you and for not getting in touch. I am angry at myself when I look at you here, when I see what you have achieved without me. To know that I missed not only your growing up but the raising of my own grandchildren. I never dreamt there were grandchildren.'

'You imagined time standing still?'

'I pushed you to the back of my mind. I tried not remember.'

'How could anyone try not to remember their children?' Ruth sounded incredulous. She could not even begin to imagine leaving Aston to raise Rebecca.

'It would take a million years to try and explain my feelings.'

Nadine sat upright.

'I can see what a good job your father has done raising you and I know that I can never take that away. But now that we have come together I would like to be part of this family again. Robert, Aston, Sharon, Steven,' she appealed to each of them in turn.

Robert's voice was gruff. 'I cannot speak for the children. But me never did haccept what you done to us an me know it will tek more than jus a likkle while for me to come to terms wid you bein back in my life.'

'We will all need time,' was all that Sharon said.

And so she had driven away after extracting a promise that she would be able to see her grandchildren again. Robert closed the door behind Sharon having told her she must make her own mind up.

'But what about you, daddy? Do you want her back in your life?'

The scent of lilacs was still strong in the spring night air wafting to meet Doris. Almost ten o'clock. Undeterred she pressed her finger firmly on the bell. Perhaps he was already in bed or maybe he was staying with one of his children. What then?

'I must speak to him tonight, I must.'

Shuffling sounds approached the door. Someone was coming.

'Robert.'

'Who dere?'

'It's me, Doris.'

'Doris?'

'Yes I need to speak to you, to see you, Robert.'

'Oh, oh, I thought you was. Jus a minute, hold on.'

She would hold on, she certainly wasn't going anywhere.

Robert was in his pyjamas, a robe and slippers. Undeterred, Doris stepped over his doorstep.

'Hello, dear.'

She took the gnarled velvety hand and drew it towards her face.

He closed the door. He slipped the bolt back on and put on the security chain.

'Come.'

'Let me take your coat.'

All thumbs and fingers, she unbuttoned it and passed it to him.

He took her hand and led her down the hallway into the lamp lit back room. Doris was certain she caught a scent of a ripening mango as she entered.

'I was jus havin a likkle nightcap. A drink o rum. Can I get you a drink? Tea? Coffee?' He paused. 'Or something else?'

'Well if it's not too much trouble. I mean, not too late.'

'Too late? Too late for what?'

He handed her a small glass and waved her to a chair. Doris sipped the amber coloured liquid.

'Oh,' she giggled. 'I've never drunk rum before.'

'Dere is always a first time,' said Robert.

He moved forward to hand her his handkerchief. Doris stood up as he approached her chair.

'A first time and plenty of time. An it not too late for us, Doris Thomas. Come here.'

He opened his arms to her. Lavender and aftershave mingled as she moved into them. And much later, his arm was around her shoulders as they walked towards the stairs.